> Buffy turned **the pages of the yearbook** until she came up with the answer. There was a full-page picture of Cordelia, all smiles and joy.

At least that's what it seemed to be. It was hard to tell. Marcie had covered the picture with wild pen scratches and drawn a hideous red crown on Cordy's head. "Just as we thought," she told Xander. "Cordelia."

As if on cue, the prom queen herself came tearing into the library, a look of sheer panic on her face. "I knew I'd find you here," she told Buffy. She seemed to have no idea she'd interrupted anything. "Buffy, I, uh, know we've had our differences, you being so weird and all, and hanging out with these—ugh—*total* losers and . . ." Cordelia looked at the expressions on the faces of Buffy and her friends. *Oops. Wrong approach.* "Well, anyway," she continued, changing tactics, "despite all that, I know you share this feeling we have for each other deep down. . . ."

"Nausea?" Willow interrupted.

Cordelia's patience had run out. "Somebody's after me!" she screamed, somewhat hysterically. "They just tried to kill Ms. Miller! And she was helping me with homework! And Mitch and Harmony! This is all about me! Me! Me!"

Xander laughed. "Wow. For once, she's right."

Buffy the Vampire Slayer™

Available from SIMON PULSE

The Cordelia Collection, Vol.1

A novelization by Nancy Krulik
Based on the hit TV series created
by Joss Whedon

Based on the teleplays "Out of Mind, Out of Sight," by Ashley Gable &
Thomas A. Swyden (story by Joss Whedon), "Some Assembly Required,"
by Ty King, and "Homecoming," by David Greenwalt.

SIMON PULSE
NEW YORK LONDON TORONTO SYDNEY SINGAPORE

First Simon Pulse edition December 2002

SIMON PULSE
An imprint of Simon & Schuster
Children's Publishing Division
1230 Avenue of the Americas
New York, NY 10020

The text of this book was set in Times.
Printed in the United States of America.
2 4 6 8 10 9 7 5 3 1
Library of Congress Control Number 2002106915
ISBN 0-7434-2746-7

For Danny

Prologue

"Take your time much?" Cordelia Chase huffed as she snatched her fresh hot latte from the hands of the bartender.

"I'm sorry," the bartender apologized with a weary sigh. The Bronze was especially crowded tonight, and she obviously wasn't interested in getting any customer attitude.

"Whatever," Cordelia replied, effectively dismissing the club worker. She took a sip of the coffee and licked a bit of white foam from her lips. Then she looked down and smoothed a wrinkle from her new red silk mini.

The bartender stood for a moment, eyeing Cordelia cautiously. *Clearly waiting for a tip.*

"Here's a tip," Cordelia quipped. "Someone with your facial shape should definitely lose the bangs."

Cordelia laughed to herself as the bewildered worker wandered off toward the other end of the coffee bar. She took a second sip of her latte, ran her perfectly manicured fingernails through her long, dark, silky hair, and snuggled back against the arm of her boyfriend *du jour,* high school baseball star Mitch Fargo.

"The Bronze is really hopping tonight," Mitch commented. He let out a slight yawn, stretched his arms, and then let his hand fall suggestively on Cordelia's thigh.

If Cordelia noticed this provocative motion, she didn't let on. She was more concerned that she and Mitch were sitting at a good angle—one in which everyone at the Bronze could see that she was currently attached to the most eligible hottie at Sunnydale High School. Only once she was completely satisfied that not only could she and Mitch be seen, but that her good side was *especially* visible from the dance floor, did Cordelia begin to relax. This was the kind of night she liked. Loud music, an adoring public, and *no trouble*.

An oogy-free evening was no easy order in Sunnydale. Disaster just seemed drawn to the town. Lately it seemed that the lifespan of a teenager attending Sunnydale High School wasn't much longer than that of an insect. Kids really did seem to be dropping like flies these days—and in some of the strangest ways. One cheerleader had recently gone up in smoke—the first case of spontaneous combustion ever in the history of Sunnydale Cheerleading. On the bright side it had cleared the way for Cordy's ascension to varsity stardom. Another girl had actually had her heart cut out (*très* yuch!) right before the talent show. Then computer geek Dave had hanged himself in the computer lab. There was also that rumor that some students had actually eaten Sunnydale High's old principal, Mr. Flutie, alive. Of course the official word was that he'd been eaten by a pack of dogs, but even *that* was *mucho* bizarro.

As far as Cordelia could see, there wasn't a whole lot connecting these *el weirdo* deaths, unless you counted the fact that there seemed to be a whole lot more trouble in Sunnydale since Buffy Summers showed up in town. It seemed that no matter where disaster struck, Buffy was always nearby.

At first Cordelia had tried to like Buffy. After all, the girl was from Los Angeles, the land of movie stars, mansions, and *so much shopping*. Cordelia'd figured that alone would make her cool. Unfortunately (and Cordelia would never admit this to anyone), she'd been *wrong* about Buffy. Buffy wasn't simply uncool, she was *über*-uncool. She'd taken to budding up with Willow Rosenberg and Xander Harris. The three of them hung out in the library, having nerd-fests with the school librarian! Once she started appearing on the scene of all these creepy incidents, Buffy's downward mobility was cemented in stone.

Cordelia bopped her head up and down slightly as she listened to the three piece band thrashing away at their instruments. She was about to suggest that she and Mitch get up and dance when she noticed three teens— a guy and two girls—walking into the club. The guy stood in the middle. He was tall, with slightly wind-blown brown hair. He'd almost be cute, Cordelia thought, except that he was wearing a flannel shirt, and Seattle grunge was *so* over. On his left was a petite redhead in a pair of low-cut jeans and a bright, fuzzy sweater. To his right was a thin blonde, dressed in black leather pants and a tank top.

"Well, there goes the neighborhood," Cordelia moaned as she stared across the dance floor at Xander, Willow, and Buffy.

"Out of Mind, Out of Sight"

Cordelia Chase flashed her bright white smile at the latest group of admirers who had gathered around her in the school hallway early Monday morning. "I just love springtime. Me in bright spring fashions," she declared, making sure her adoring audience noticed her new sky-blue, V-neck sweater with matching skirt.

Mitch had his own ideas about the joys of the season. "Spring training," he mused aloud.

"Me at the end-of-school dance," Cordelia continued, seeming not to have heard Mitch speak at all.

"The end of school," Cordelia's best friend Harmony chimed in.

"Definitely my favorite time of the year," Cordelia reiterated with a confident smile as she began to stroll slowly to class. Cordelia never liked to rush through the halls. She wanted to make sure that everyone had a chance to notice her.

And admire her they did. Students standing at their lockers turned to look at the campus queen and her followers as the passed by. Cordelia appeared to barely acknowledge the presence of these lesser beings, but in her mind she took note of every one of their glances of longing. Cordelia knew that all the girls wanted to be her and all the boys wanted to date her.

As the group of friends strolled past a poster that read CAST YOUR VOTE ON THURSDAY FOR MAY QUEEN! Cordelia was reminded that she had a fitting that very afternoon for the gown she was going to wear to Sunnydale High's annual Spring Fling. "I am, of course, having my dress specially made," she told Mitch and Harmony. "Off the rack gives me hives."

Mitch smiled mischievously. "Let me guess. Blue, like your eyes."

"My eyes are *hazel*, Helen Keller," she snapped, scowling.

"You two will look so fine together in the May Queen photo," Harmony interrupted before Sunnydale's premiere—albeit transient—couple could start bickering. Harmony was trying to promote, well, *harmony*.

Cordelia beamed at the thought of being photographed as the May Queen. "Well, technically, I haven't been elected May Queen yet." Her voice dripped with false modesty.

As if on cue, Mitch and Harmony erupted into laughter. Elections were a total formality.

The trio's banter was broken as the library doors burst open. Buffy Summers came flying out of the room at top speed, slamming directly into Cordelia and Mitch. An avalanche of books, papers, and little wooden sticks of all shapes and sizes exploded from her backpack to the floor below.

"Behold the weirdness," Cordelia announced coldly.

Buffy hurried to gather the mess together. "You're probably wondering what I'm doing with all this stuff," she murmured nervously as she stuffed one of the sticks into her pack.

Cordelia rolled her eyes. "Wow. I'm not." *Duh.*

"It's actually for show and tell," Buffy explained, ignoring Cordelia's obvious disinterest. "For history class, Mr. Giles has this, like, hobby. A hobby of collecting stuff. Which he lent me. For show and tell. Did I mention it's for history class?"

Mitch, Cordelia, and Harmony stared at Buffy in amazement. How had the girl managed to say all that without taking a breath? And could they care less?

Buffy looked at their bemused faces and sighed. She'd sounded like a total babbling idiot.

"She is always hanging with the creepy librarian in the creepy library," Harmony noted.

Mitch grimaced. "Ew. Libraries. All those books. What's up with that?"

Cordelia giggled and took Mitch's arm in hers. Together, the odds-on favorite for May King and Queen walked off down the hall with Harmony, their blonde, pony-tailed lady-in-waiting, not far behind.

• • •

Buffy watched them strut away with a sense of longing. Yes, Cordelia was totally shallow and Buffy knew she shouldn't feel bad about being an outsider to "the Cordettes." Buffy of all people knew there were more important things in this world than being popular. Saving the world from evil for example.

That was, after all, Buffy's prime purpose of late. Sunnydale High was located on the Hellmouth—the center of mystical gravity to which things gravitated that you might not find anywhere else. Horrible things like vampires. Buffy was a vampire slayer—faster, stronger, and more resilient than normal humans. She alone was chosen by the Powers That Be to combat the evils of the the world. Which was kind of cool, except that almost nightly she was forced to face unspeakable evil—and to slay or be slain.

Not a life for the faint hearted—or, for that matter, anyone with an actual social life.

Back in L.A., Buffy had been the typical popular blond cheerleader—not unlike Cordelia. But being called had changed all of that.

Being a slayer was an awesome responsibility. One that Mr. Rupert Giles, or "that creepy librarian," as Harmony had put it, felt Buffy should spend far more time preparing for. Giles was a watcher. It was his responsibility to train and prepare his slayer for whatever horrors might await her.

It was all pretty heady stuff. But somehow, Buffy couldn't help but wish for some semblance of her old life—her *normal* life—back. It'd be such a break to converse about the merits of Prada shoes versus Steve

Madden, instead of figuring out how sharp a stake needed to be to penetrate an especially chubby vampire's heart.

But there was no time to consider that right now. Buffy had only three minutes to get across campus to her Algebra class.

Boredom, thy name is Shakespeare, Willow thought glumly. While Buff was busy decoding equations, she and Xander were trying to unlock the mysteries of *Merchant of Venice* in their lit class. But Willow was having a hard time getting the teacher to engage. As was not uncommon, Cordelia had managed to suck up most of Ms. Miller's attention.

"'If you prick us, do we not bleed? If you tickle us do we not laugh?'" their teacher, Ms. Miller, recited with overwhelming enthusiasm. "'If you poison us do we not die? And if you wrong us, shall we not revenge?'"

The teacher stopped and looked around the classroom at twenty sets of glazed, confused eyes. "Okay, so talk to me people," she urged. "How does what Shylock says here about being Jewish relate to our discussion— about the anger of the outcast at society?"

Most of the students sank down lower in their chairs, secretly praying that Ms. Miller might magically forget they existed. In fact, only Willow and Cordelia raised their hands.

Ms. Miller smiled at the pretty brunette. "Cordelia?"

Willow lowered her hand, disappointed but not surprised. Ms. Miller wasn't the first teacher to fall victim to Cordelia's charm mechanisms. She wouldn't be the last, either.

"What's Shylock saying?" Ms. Miller continued.

"How about 'color me totally self-involved'?" Cordelia declared. "With Shylock it's whine, whine, whine, like the whole world is about him! He acts like it's justice, him getting a pound of Antonio's flesh. It's not justice. It's yicky."

Ms. Miller looked out across the room. "But has Shylock suffered? What's his place in society?"

"Well, everyone looks down on him," Willow interjected.

Cordelia rolled her eyes. "That's such a twinkie defense!" she countered. "Shylock should get over himself. People who think their problems are so huge craze me. Like the time I sort of ran over this girl on her bike. It was the most traumatizing event of my life, and she's trying to make it all about her leg. Like my pain meant nothing."

Xander and Willow exchanged a glance. Surely Ms. Miller would see through that load of crap, right?

Not exactly. "Cordelia's raised an interesting point here," the teacher began as the bell rang. "Which we will pursue next time."

At the sound of the bell, the students emerged from their Shakespeare-inspired haze, leaped up, and dashed out of the room. Only Cordelia stopped at the teacher's desk before moving on.

"Ms. Miller?" she asked sweetly.

The teacher smiled at her. "Some good observations today, Cordelia. Always exciting to know someone's actually done the reading."

Willow scowled. *I did the reading.*

"I wanted to talk to you about my final paper," Cordelia explained. "I'm real unfocused. I have all these ideas, and I'm pretty sure they all contradict each other."

Ms. Miller glanced down at her desk and nodded. "I have your outline here somewhere," she said. "Why don't you stop in after school tomorrow and we can go over it?"

"That's great, thanks," Cordelia agreed. She strode confidently out the door and into the hall.

If Cordelia had been sensitive to anything other than her own needs and wants, she might have noticed an eerie aura looming in the air just outside Ms. Miller's room. The hallway appeared empty, and yet there was someone there, watching ominously as Cordelia started off toward her next class.

Here she is, Miss Popularity. The unseen stalker quietly hummed the words to herself then sighed miserably. *It must be nice to be so perfect. Or at least* appear *to be perfect. Too bad the boneheads in this school can't view her the way I do. None of these losers can see past her perfect little nose, her big eyes, her coiffed hair, or that skinny little waist.*

Make that waste. *Cordelia Chase is a total waste of a human being.*

It was only minutes later that Mitch Fargo walked out of the shower in the boys' locker room and began getting dressed.

"You going to the Bronze?" one of Mitch's teammates asked.

Mitch shoved his leg into his pants and nodded. "Later. I'm picking up my tux first. Got to look sharp for the big 'dig."

His teammate grinned. "That's right. Gotta look good to be on Cordelia's arm."

Mitch shot his buddy a conspiratory smile. "It's not her arm I'm looking to be on," he laughed.

His pal laughed heartily and then headed out of the locker room, leaving Mitch there alone.

Suddenly an eerie giggle rang through the locker room. The shrill laughter sent a chill through Mitch's body. It sounded almost inhuman.

"Who's there?" Mitch called out. He waited for someone to answer, but there was no response. No movement. Nothing.

The giggling started again—louder and wilder now, almost maniacal.

"Okay, fun time's over," Mitch shouted angrily. "Come out!"

There was no answer to his call. From the corner of his eye, Mitch spotted a baseball bat perched atop the lockers. He reached out. But before Mitch could grasp it, the wooden bat rose into the air on its own. Mitch looked up just in time to see the bat come crashing down right onto his head.

Mitch stumbled dizzily against the lockers. Through his bewildered haze he spotted the bat floating above his head. He scurried to get away as the seemingly possessed bat aimed for his skull once again. He ducked, and the bat slammed into the metal lockers. As the sound of crashing metal echoed through the empty locker room, Mitch tried to scramble away, but he was too dazed from the hit to move quickly. The bat came down once more. The force sent Mitch reeling toward the ground.

Mitch did not get up again. He lay there, still on the ground, a pool of blood slowly forming around him.

"Remember who to vote for for May Queen," Cordelia reminded one of her classmates as she handed him a delicate chocolate wrapped in gold. "As in, me."

Cordelia made her way down the hall, handing chocolates out to everyone in her path. Finding Harmony, she held up one of the small chocolates. "Isn't this the *bomb*? I'm *such* the campaign strategist."

Harmony eyed the gold wrapper carefully. "*C*," she noted. "For Cordelia?"

"No, *C* for Wilma. Of course it's for Cordelia, little brain. This way people will associate me, Cordelia, with something sweet."

She handed out a few more of the candies to passersby. As Buffy drifted by, Cordelia reached out toward her and then quickly snapped the chocolate back. "I don't think I need the loony fringe vote," she decided.

Buffy watched as Cordelia and Harmony strolled off, making no attempt to mask their distaste for her. "I don't even like chocolate," she called after them. "Well, that was the lamest comeback of our times," she muttered to herself, embarrassed.

"Hey!" Xander greeted Buffy as he and Willow came up behind her in the hall. "What's Cordelia up to?"

"Bribery. She's desperate to be May Queen."

Xander laughed. "Cordelia, man . . . she does love titles."

Willow giggled, knowing exactly what Xander was thinking of. "Oh, God, remember in sixth grade . . . the field trip? When Cordelia . . ."

Xander cracked up. "Right. Right. The guy with the antlers on his belt . . ."

Willow put her hands on an imaginary belt and did an amazingly ridiculous imitation of a John Wayne type. "Be my deputy."

Xander nearly collapsed with laughter. "And she had the . . . with the hat . . ."

"The hat!" Willow exclaimed.

"Oh, man . . . ," Xander agreed.

"Okay, it's fun that we're speaking in tongues," Buffy snapped, still smarting from her non-exchange with Cordelia.

Willow bit her lip in an attempt to stop laughing. "I'm sorry."

Xander choked back a few chuckles of his own. "It was, we had this . . . you had to be there."

"It's not even funny," Willow assured Buffy. "Cordelia just has a history of trying too hard."

"What kind of moron would be May Queen anyway?" Xander wondered.

"I was," Buffy said quietly, looking down.

"You what?" Xander made no attempt to hide his surprise.

"At my old school."

Xander could feel the warmth flowing into his cheeks as the embarrassment caused him to blush, big time. "So, the good kind of moron would do that. The non-moron I mean. I'll be in a quiet place now."

Buffy thought back to her days at her old school. *Back when I was normal girl. Buffy non-slayer.* "I mean, we didn't call it May Queen, but we had the dance, the coronation, and all that stuff. It was nice," she added wistfully.

Xander flashed a compassionate smile. "Well, you don't need that stuff now. You've got us."

Willow could no longer contain the laughter she'd been holding in. She burst into giggles. "Be my deputy," she repeated.

Suddenly one of the school's baseball players burst his way into the hall, interrupting Willow's comedy routine. "Guys! Come on!" he shouted wildly. Instantly a crowd of kids started running with him toward the locker room. But before anyone could make their way to the scene of the crime, Mr. Snyder, the school principal blocked their way.

"Somebody's wailed on Mitch!" the baseball player told the rapidly growing mob. "I think he's—"

"Dead?" Mr. Snyder interjected nervously. "Of course not. Dead! What are you, ghouls? There are no dead students here! *This week,*" he added under his breath. "Now clear back. Make room, all of you!"

The kids watched as a pair of EMTs wheeled Mitch from the locker room on a gurney. The big sports star looked small and fragile under the cold white hospital sheet. His nose looked broken, and there were patches of dried blood all over his skin.

Looking at him, it would be easy to think that this had been the work of some human with a grudge. But

Buffy knew better than to assume that humans were behind any of the violence in Sunnydale. Slayer mode took over.

"Mitch, what happened?" she asked as they wheeled the baseball player away.

"I don't know," Mitch mumbled painfully. "I heard something. I tried to grab a bat . . . and it hit me."

"What hit you?"

Mitch's eyes stared into Buffy's. "The bat," he told her as he lay in shock on the stretcher. "By itself. Thing was floating! Knocked me out. . . ."

As the paramedics carried Mitch out to the ambulance, Buffy glanced knowingly at Willow and Xander. "I better check out the scene." Quickly she started for the locker room.

Unfortunately, Mr. Snyder had other ideas. "Where do you think you're going?" he demanded.

Buffy was amazed at just how much the small, beady-eyed principal resembled a rat when faced with situations like this. "Um . . . Mitch wanted me to get . . . his comb," Buffy stammered. "He likes his comb." *Okay, not the best excuse, but maybe it would work.*

No such luck. "I don't think Mitch needs his comb right now," Principal Snyder snarled. "I think Mitch needs medical attention and you need to stay away from the crime scene. You're always sticking your nose in—"

Fortunately Willow was quick to make with the distraction. "What did you say?" she remarked, loud enough for the principal to hear. "Mitch is gonna sue the school?"

That got Mr. Snyder's attention—big time. "Sue? Who?" he asked nervously.

"Well, his dad is the most powerful lawyer in Sunnydale," Xander told Willow.

"Hold on! What have you two heard?" Mr. Snyder asked nervously, turning his attention away from Buffy and the locker room.

"Mitch's dad," Xander said. "The lawyer. You've never heard of him?"

"Other lawyers call him The Beast," Willow added.

As Mr. Snyder interrogated Willow and Xander, Buffy quickly sneaked behind him. She mouthed a silent *thank you* to her two pals and slipped away quietly. *Well done, Scoobies.*

The boys' locker room was eerily silent. It was completely abandoned now, but Buffy quickly noted definite signs of a vicious struggle. Lockers were dented, and a baseball bat sat squarely in the center of a smear of Mitch's blood. Buffy reached out her foot and hesitantly kicked at it with her thick leather boot. The bat rolled across the floor—just like any other normal baseball bat might. *Okay, so not possessed then.*

Buffy turned and looked around the room. All the lockers were shut, except for a group of four in a nearby row. That seemed curious. Quickly she crossed the room and peered inside one of the lockers. *Empty.* Quietly, Buffy shut the locker. That's when she saw the big, red, K spray-painted on the door.

K? Buffy wondered silently. *What's that about?* Buffy stared at the three adjacent locker doors for a moment and then slowly closed them one by one.

A single red letter was spray-painted on each of the locker doors.

LOOK

"'Look'? That's all it said?" Willow asked Buffy that afternoon during lunch. She licked a spot of ketchup from her fingers.

"Look at what?" Xander wondered aloud. "Look at Mitch?"

Buffy shrugged. "Maybe. All I know is it's a message."

"And?" Xander asked.

"And monsters don't usually send messages," Buffy explained to him. "It's pretty much, 'kill, crush, destroy.' This is different."

Just then Giles strolled over toward the table where the three were sitting. "I'd say you're right," he told Buffy as he took a seat at the small round table.

"I love it when you say that." Buffy laughed lightly. "Any theories?"

"It's a bit of a puzzle," Giles admitted in his oh-so-proper British accent. "I haven't actually heard of someone being attacked by a baseball bat."

"Maybe it's a *vampire* bat," Xander interjected playfully. Then, noting that he was the only one laughing at his joke, "I'm alone with that one," he admitted sheepishly.

Giles rolled his eyes, but otherwise ignored Xander. "Well, assuming the bat itself is not possessed, there are a few possibilities that bear investigating. Someone with telekinesis—the power to move objects at will—some invisible creature, or possibly a poltergeist."

"A ghost?" Willow asked, her voice sliding nervously up the scale.

Giles nodded. "Yes. An angry one."

"Yeah, I'll say," Buffy seconded. "It was a real scene in that locker room."

"So if it's a ghost, we're talking about a dead kid?" Willow asked.

"I suppose so," Buffy agreed. "Willow, why don't you compile a list of kids who've died or are missing. It's a start."

"And I'll research all the possibilities," Giles added. "Ghosts included. Xander, may I count on your help there?"

Xander frowned. He hated this part of the slaying scene. "What, there's homework now?" he asked.

"It's all part of the glamorous world of vampire slaying," Buffy teased.

Xander scowled. "Well, what are you going to be doing?" he demanded.

"Finding out what I can about Mitch," Buffy replied. "This attack wasn't random."

"Well, I think I should do that part," Xander told her.

Buffy shrugged. "Fine. Ask around. Talk to his friends. Talk to . . . *Cordelia*."

That didn't sound any less torturous than working in the library. In fact, it sounded pretty awful. He turned to Giles. "So, research, huh?"

While Buffy and her friends were busy chowing down soggy school sandwiches, Harmony and Cordelia were in the upper quad hall, talking about the fate of Cordelia's prom date. The girls could easily have been a picture in a clothing catalogue—Cordy in her sky-blue sweater and long brown hair that curled just enough. Harmony, with her blonde ponytail wrapped in a green bow that accented the trim on her light blue jacket. Their animated faces were close together, framed by an open archway in the upper quad.

"You weren't in fifth period," Harmony noted.

Cordelia took a sip of water from a nearby fountain. "I went to the hospital," she explained.

Harmony nodded understandingly. "Mitch. How is he? Will he be okay?"

Cordelia nodded slowly. "The doctor said he's fine. He'll be sent home tomorrow." She blinked away a few distraught tears. "Oh, you should have seen him—lying there. All black and blue . . ."

Harmony stared at her friend with amazement. She'd never known Cordelia to show such pity and caring for another human being.

"How's he going to look in our prom pictures?" Cordelia asked Harmony, her voice slowly rising to panic level. "How will I ever be able to show them to anyone?"

Harmony put her arm around Cordelia. "They can do wonderful things with airbrushes these days," she assured her.

"You think?" Cordelia asked hopefully.

The two girls were so caught up in their moment of worry that they didn't notice that someone had joined them in the hallway. The silent observer stood there, quietly watching the girls. She wasn't surprised that Cordelia didn't sense her presence in the hall. The cheerleader never noticed anyone but herself.

The image of the two picture-perfect girls standing by the water fountain reminded her of something that had happened six months ago, in this very spot. A memory she'd kept buried for a long time.

Cordy and Harmony had been standing by the fountain, talking about Mitch and his old girlfriend. As usual the girls had seemed flawless—Cordy with her perfectly coiffed do, and Harmony with her long, flowing blond hair. They seemed unapproachable. Which of course, they were.

"Did you see Mitch?" The quiet, mousy passerby had heard Cordelia ask Harmony. "He broke up with Wendy like eight seconds ago and he's already nosing around."

"It's shameless," Harmony had responded.

"In the spring, if he makes varsity baseball, maybe I'll take him on a test drive." Then Cordelia had started to laugh—until she noticed the short-haired, freckled girl staring at her.

"Hi, guys," the girl had said, hoping for at least a morsel of attention from Cordy and Harmony.

What she'd gotten was sheer disdain. "What do you want?" Cordelia had barked at her.

At the time, the cheerleader's words had stung as strongly as if Cordelia had slapped the quiet onlooker across the face. But today, as she watched Cordy and Harmony continue their superficial banter, that same quiet, mousy girl knew that Cordelia could no longer hurt her. In fact, the tables had turned. The unknown observer was on top now. She could make life miserable for Cordelia . . . *any time she wanted to.*

That knowledge made her smile, especially since at the moment, Cordy had no idea that she had anything to fear—other than going to the prom with a bruised, and therefore unattractive, date.

The observer followed noiselessly behind as Cordy and Harmony headed toward the stairs to go to their next class.

"I just hope somebody can prop him up long enough to take the picture," Cordelia sighed.

"Cordelia, can I talk to you?" The conversation was interrupted by Buffy's shouts down the long hallway.

Cordelia and Harmony stopped near the top of the stairs and turned toward Buffy.

"Oh great," Cordelia remarked, dismissing Buffy as though she were a flea.

"Why is she always—," Harmony began. Then, suddenly, inexplicably, she rocketed backwards and tumbled down the stairs. Harmony's slim body ricocheted off the banister and landed in a heap at the foot of the stairs.

Mr. Snyder was passing by and heard Harmony's agonizing moans. "For heaven's sake!" he shouted out as he saw the fallen girl. "Clear back everyone! Give her some air!" He pointed to a student on the stairs. "You! School nurse! Now!" he ordered.

Quickly, Cordelia and Buffy raced to Harmony's aid. Harmony clutched at the leg of her light blue pant suit and moaned again. "My ankle. I think it's broken."

Cordelia wrung her hands nervously but didn't say anything.

"What happened?" Buffy asked Harmony.

Mr. Snyder shot Buffy an angry look. "Hey! Who's the principal here?" he asked her accusingly. Turning toward Cordelia, he asked pointedly. "What happened?"

"She just fell!" Cordelia exclaimed. We were standing at the top of the stairs and she just fell! All by herself!"

"No. I was pushed!" Harmony insisted.

Buffy didn't doubt for a moment that Harmony was pushed. The question was, *by whom.* As she ran off, Buffy heard Harmony shriek.

"Don't sue," Principal Snyder begged.

Hearing a strange, evil giggle behind her, the Slayer spun around and came face to face with . . . absolutely no one.

Something bizarre was definitely going down here. That was made even more clear when a nearby door opened and shut—all by itself. That was the kind of invitation a slayer couldn't resist. Buffy hurried toward the hallway.

Whoa. How weird was this? Buffy had entered the hallway only seconds after the door had closed, and yet, whoever had opened the door was gone. Or at least they appeared to be gone. "Anyone here?" Buffy asked tentatively.

There was no answer. Suddenly someone—or something—brushed past Buffy with a force so great, it almost knocked her to floor. "Hey? Who is . . . ," Buffy began as she scrambled to regain her footing. But before she could get the sentence out, another doorway opened and closed. Quickly, Buffy raced through the door.

The second door led to the band room. Buffy's green eyes scanned the room quickly; music stands, pieces of sheet music, guitar picks, and instrument cases were all in place. But there was no one else in the room. At least not that Buffy could see. *Okay, so pretty much invisible person. Got it.*

Buffy called out to whoever—or whatever—might hear her. "Okay, I know someone's here," she said, using her best nonthreatening voice. "I just want to talk to you."

There was still no answer. In fact there was no sign at all that anyone else was in the room—except for one small detail. One of the ceiling tiles in the band room had been moved, revealing the empty crawl space above. The Slayer lay in wait, her body at the ready, her mind wondering if any second now, someone was about to pounce on her from above.

But no one appeared, and it became clear that Buffy wouldn't be battling any supernatural beings at the moment. She left the room with a sigh. What ever had been there was obviously gone.

Or not.

Actually someone was still there—she just didn't want to be found . . . yet. Not until she'd had a chance to play around with Cordelia's perfect life for a while.

As the door slammed shut, Cordelia's unknown stalker reached out and slid the ceiling tile back into place.

It was best to stay hidden—for now.

• • •

"Giles, have you ever touched a ghost?" Buffy asked as the Scooby Squad gathered together outside of Sunnydale High at the end of the school day.

It might have seemed like an odd question to one of the hundreds of kids who were rushing out of the school building, but the Scooby Squad was pretty innocuous in the high school hierarchy. No one would ever think of eavesdropping on them. So the three students and the librarian were able to walk freely across the lawn at the front of the school as they discussed their latest supernatural crisis.

Giles shook his head. "No, I haven't. From what I've read, having a ghost pass through you is a singular experience. It's a cold, amorphous feeling; makes your hair stand up."

Buffy nodded slightly as she absorbed this new information. "Okay, this is my problem," she told the others. "I touched the thing. It didn't go through me, it bumped into me. And it wasn't cold."

Xander looked at her curiously. "So this means, what?" he asked. "That we're talking about an invisible person?"

Buffy nodded. "A girl. She laughed."

"A girl on campus with the power to turn invisible," Giles stated slowly.

"Man, that is so cool!" Xander exclaimed.

Willow looked at him strangely. "Cool?"

"I'd give anything to be able to turn invisible," Xander assured her. Seeing the look Buffy had given him, he added quickly, "Well, I wouldn't be beating people up. I'd use my power to protect the girls' locker room."

Giles wisely ignored Xander's burst of hormones. "It probably is an awfully heady experience, having that ability," he mused.

"So how'd she get it? Is she a witch? 'Cause we can fight a witch," Willow added positively.

Xander thought for a moment. "Greek myths talk about cloaks of invisibility, but they're usually just for the gods," he told the others.

Where'd that come from? Buffy, Willow, and Giles made absolutely no attempt to hide their amazement at Xander's pronouncement.

Xander raised his eyebrows playfully and grinned. "Research boy comes through with the knowledge," he congratulated himself.

It might have been great research, but Buffy wasn't convinced that the info fit the situation. "This girl's sort of petty for a god," she explained.

"She's got a grudge," Willow agreed. "But why Harmony?"

"Harmony and *Mitch*," Xander reminded her. "And the common denominator there is . . ."

"Cordelia." Buffy finished his thought.

"So what now?" Willow asked Buffy.

"First thing tomorrow, pull up that missing kids list," Buffy suggested.

Willow nodded. "Got it. I'll see you then."

"Good."

"See ya," Xander called as he hurried to get into step with Willow. "Why don't you have dinner at our place?" he asked the petite redhead as they walked off. "Mom's making her famous phone call to the Chinese place."

Willow laughed. "Again? Xander, do you guys *have* a stove?"

Buffy stood beside Giles and watched enviously as her two friends headed home. Although everyone in the Scooby Squad had faced their share of danger in the past few months, life was still easier for Willow and Xander than it was for Buffy. They could go home and enjoy an evening of laughs and lo mein, but a slayer's work was never done.

Giles turned to her. "I'll start looking into ways to decloak an invisible someone. And you?"

"I think Cordelia's gonna be working on the May Queen decorations. There might be some action. It's time for me to start the hunt."

"And how do you propose to hunt someone you can't see?" Giles asked. "You may actually have to start listening to people," he added sarcastically.

"Very funny, " Buffy replied.

"I thought so," Giles agreed.

Watcher one, slayer zero.

That night, Buffy returned to Sunnydale High. The building was quiet, cold, and deserted. The name Sunnydale seemed oddly inappropriate at this time of night; rather than sunny, the halls were dimly lit and shadowy.

Buffy was taking no chances. She had no idea where this invisible girl might be hiding—or what plans she had in store. Buffy's fully-stocked slayer bag was slung over her shoulder, with knives, stakes, and other hunting gear at the ready. Her heart pounded slightly, her body filled with adrenaline, her every sense fully alert and her every step carefully placed. Total slayer mode.

"Hello? Invisible person?" she called out into the empty hallway.

There was no response.

"I know you're here," Buffy continued. "I know I can't see you. It's a good trick. Care to teach it to me?"

This time Buffy could hear someone giggling in the shadows. It was coming from a classroom just down the hall. A bright light beamed out from the open doorway. Quickly Buffy moved toward the light and peered inside.

Buffy sighed heavily as she realized that the laughter had not come from the invisible girl. It had come from one of Cordelia's many admirers, all of whom were currently gathered together in the classroom making cheery springtime decorations for the prom. As usual, Cordelia stood in the center of the room, enjoying the adoration of her followers. Two of her friends were helping her measure the hem on her new shimmering peach satin and taffeta and sequined gown. As she spun around, the material seemed to sparkle in the light. Buffy had to admit that Cordelia was going to look beautiful. Like a princess. Make that a *queen*—the May Queen.

Buffy looked down at her own black leather vampire hunting jacket and sighed. She felt more than a twinge of jealousy as she watched Cordelia and her friends laughing with anticipation. Dresses. Dances. Things that other girls got to experience. Normal girls.

For them, the night of the dance would be magical, filled with romance and music. For Buffy, most nights were filled with vampires, witches, and now invisible girls. Creepy crawly things. Things of the Bad.

Suddenly Buffy heard another sound coming from far off, somewhere deep in the school. This was not laughter. This was music—a single flute playing an eerie song. Buffy stood there alone in the shadowy hallway listening to the mournful tune. It was the saddest sound she'd ever heard.

Alone in the library, busy with late night research, Giles froze. The strains of a gentle flute melody had caught his attention. But the music stopped as suddenly as it had begun. Giles shrugged and resumed his research, but only for a second. A noise in the otherwise empty room told him someone was in the library with him. Someone uninvited.

"Who's there?" Giles asked, trying to hide the edginess in his voice. Slowly the librarian peered behind the stacks of books . . . and saw no one. As he passed by the books, he checked his reflection in one of the library's darkened windows. Only his own face stared back at him.

But Giles was not alone. As he turned again he came face to face with a tall, dark man, who looked no more than twenty or twenty-one. Giles knew otherwise. This was no man. This was Angel, a 241-year-old vampire and the object of Buffy's affection. Giles glanced back toward the window. Again, only his own face was reflected there.

"Of course," Giles muttered aloud. "Vampires cast no reflection." He looked toward the door, mentally gauging a path to the nearest exit.

"Don't worry," Angel assured him. "I'm not here to eat."

Giles nodded. "Buffy told me you don't feed on humans anymore."

"Not for a long while," Angel agreed.

"Is that why you're here?" Giles asked. "To see her?"

Angel shook his head. "I can't," he said, unable to hide the anguish in his voice. "It's too hard for me to be around her."

Ah, the irony. Giles's voice became more tender. "A vampire in love with a slayer," he mused aloud. "It's rather poetic, in a maudlin sort of way. Well, what can I do for you?"

"I know you've been researching the master."

Giles nodded. "The Vampire King. Yes, I'm trying to learn all I can about him . . . for the day when Buffy must face him. I haven't learned much, I'm afraid."

Angel stared thoughtfully into Giles's eye, making sure that the librarian would heed his words. "Things I've heard lately . . . from . . ." Angel's voice grew dark and ominous. "From things you wouldn't care to meet . . . Something's already in motion—something big. But I don't know what. You've read all the Slayer lore there is, right?"

Giles shook his head. "I've studied all the extant volumes, of course," he explained. "But the most important books of Slayer prophecy have been lost. The *Tiberius Manifesto,* the *Pergamum Codex* . . ."

"The *Codex* . . ." Angel repeated.

"It was reputed to contain the most complete prophecies about the Slayer's role in the End Times. But the book was lost in the fifteenth century," he added ruefully.

Angel shook his head. "Not lost. *Misplaced.* I can get it."

Giles looked at him with amazement and sincere gratitude. "That would be very helpful." He glanced down at the pile of books beside him. "My own volumes seem to be useless of late."

Angel lifted one of the massive tomes. It was ancient and dusty, and obviously had been read many times. He examined the leather spine with curiosity. The book didn't look familiar to him. "*Legends of Vishnu?*"

"There's an invisible girl terrorizing the school," Giles explained.

Angel shrugged and put down the book. "Oh. That's not really my area of expertise."

"Nor mine, I'm afraid," Giles responded. "It's a fascinating thought. By all accounts a wonderful power to have."

Angel wasn't so sure. "I don't know. . . . Looking in the mirror every day and seeing nothing there—it's an overrated pleasure."

Giles heard the painful longing in Angel's tone but said nothing as he followed the vampire's glance at the darkened window. The librarian turned to say something kind to the struggling vampire, but he had already disappeared into the night.

• • •

The next afternoon, most of the school had gathered in the quad, eagerly awaiting the announcement of the winner of the May Queen competition. In fact, the only person not eagerly awaiting Cordelia's victory speech was the silent onlooker who'd been trailing the once and future queen.

She was in a nearby girls' room, recalling yet another dismal meeting with the object of her scorn. The moment couldn't have meant much to Cordy. Probably hadn't even registered on her radar screen. But to this girl, it had been a mortifying turning point in her life.

The quiet outsider remembered it as though it were yesterday. Cordelia, Harmony, and another of the Cordettes had been busy primping in the mirror and laughing about the horrors of the older generation. They were so involved in their conversation that they hadn't even noticed there was a fourth girl in the bathroom—a girl they considered the human equivalent of wallpaper.

"God, I am never sitting through one of those alumni lectures again," Cordelia had laughed. "Two hours of 'My Trek Through Nepal.' Hello! There's nobody caring."

"Did you see his toupee?" the quiet outsider had interjected. "It looked like a cabbage."

Cordelia didn't even acknowledge her presence. "And those slides," she continued. "'That's a mountain. Yes, that's a mountain too. Now let's look at mountains.'"

Harmony had laughed at her friend's dead-on

imitation of the dull speaker. "I swear he only had three slides and he just used them over and over," she agreed.

"Did you guys notice his toupee—," the onlooker had asked again.

For the first time, Harmony had seemed to notice that there was a fourth person in the bathroom. She turned toward her and spat out, "We're talking, okay?"

As the three popular friends had left the bathroom, Cordelia'd giggled. "Oh! And did you guys check out the extreme toupee? Yeah, that's realistic. It looked like a cabbage."

Now, as she stood there, alone in the bathroom, Cordelia's nemesis strengthened her resolve to make sure that the new May Queen would recognize her existence.

She wasn't going to have any choice in the matter.

"Thank you for making the right choice, for showing how much you love me."

The group of gathered students cheered wildly at Cordy's words.

Buffy arrived at the quad just in time to hear Cordelia making her acceptance speech. She pushed her way through the crowd of adoring students. The scene was surreal: a bunch of well-dressed sheep baaing their approval to their queen.

Buffy breathed a silent sigh of relief as Willow and Xander joined her in the crowd. At last, friendly faces!

"Being this popular isn't just my right," Cordelia assured the crowd. "It's my responsibility, and I want you to know I take it seriously."

Buffy, Willow, and Xander looked at one another, laughing silently at what only they seemed to realize was a joke. But by turning away, they missed Cordelia stumbling slightly on the platform, as though someone had shoved right past her, unnoticed.

"Giles said you'd be here," Xander told Buffy. "*Why* are you being here?"

"Last night was a bust," Buffy explained. "But I still think Cordy's the key here."

Willow handed Buffy a stack of freshly printed papers. "The dead and missing girl list," she explained. "They've mostly stayed missing. I pulled their classes, activities, medical records . . ."

"Good work," Buffy complimented her.

Willow looked back up by the stage. She noticed two men lurking in the shadows behind the bushes. They were dressed in black and wore extremely shiny leather shoes. They almost looked like the secret service agents who trailed the president. Very *Men in Black*. "Has Cordelia hired bodyguards or something?" she murmured.

Xander glanced over toward the men, but Buffy was engrossed in the new list. "Whoa. Check it out. The most recent one, Marcie Ross, disappeared six months ago."

"I don't know her," Xander said.

"Me neither," Willow echoed.

Buffy scanned the information sheet. "Well, her only activity was band. She played the flute." She looked away as her mind digested the information.

"So?" Willow prodded.

"I heard a flute last night," Buffy explained. "And it was the band room where I lost Miss Invisible yesterday. This tracks. I've got a free now. I'll check it out."

"Okay," Xander agreed as he and Willow headed off toward the school building. "We'll see you after geometry."

As Buffy wandered off in search of the invisible girl, she could still hear Cordelia speaking to the masses. "So come to my coronation at the Bronze for an evening you'll never forget."

As Cordy droned on and on, Buffy cautiously made her way back to the band room in the hopes of meeting the invisible girl. She entered the room quietly and circled carefully, keeping her eyes peeled for any signs of another human. The light through the window was bright. In the stream of sunlight, Buffy could see a thin ribbon of dust falling from the corner of the ceiling. She looked up. Once again, the same tile was slightly askew. The Slayer carefully climbed up the band room shelves, pushed back the tile, and poked her head up into the hollow in the ceiling.

It was dark inside the crawl space; the only light came from behind a window fan that blew dry, stale air throughout what was apparently the invisible girl's nest. Buffy pulled herself up through the hole, taking care not to disturb any of the wires that hung perilously from the top of the lair.

As she emerged from the hole in the ceiling, Buffy looked around in amazement. The room was small and cramped, but it had everything a teen could need:

blankets and pillows, junk food, and books. Atop one of the blankets lay a single silver flute and a few scattered sheets of music. Buffy crouched down and picked up a small brown teddy bear. Gently, she stroked the creature's soft, furry ear. There was something so sad about the solo stuffed toy. Something wistful, *mournful*—like the flute music she'd heard the night before.

Buffy reached down and grabbed a yearbook that was hidden among the other items. She opened the cover and looked down at the name written across the front page. "Marcie Ross," she read quietly. "So it is you." Buffy opened the book and began to read the messages that other Sunnydale students had scribbled on the pages. She was so engrossed in looking at the yearbook that she failed to notice a sharp knife hovering dangerously behind her, ready to stab if Buffy came to close to the invisible person waving it.

But Buffy went nowhere near Marcie Ross. Instead she took the yearbook and silently left Marcie's lair.

"Cordelia, could you possibly be on time?" Ms. Miller asked incredulously. The teacher was grading papers in her classroom, awaiting Cordelia, who was coming to discuss her Shakespeare report. She barely even looked up when she heard the door to her classroom open. There was no answer . . . and no one at the door. Ms. Miller shrugged. She must've been mistaken. The teacher looked down and continued grading papers. Then suddenly she heard a high-pitched, almost maniacal giggle coming from behind her. "Who's there?" she asked nervously.

But there were no more sounds. Instead someone grabbed the teacher from behind and with frightening speed whipped a plastic bag over her head. Ms. Miller thrashed wildly, trying to battle her invisible attacker, but it was no use. In a matter of seconds the English teacher collapsed on to her desk.

It was at that very moment that Cordelia walked into the classroom. She found her teacher passed out in her chair, her face turning blue within the confines of the plastic bag. Cordelia raced to the desk and instinctively yanked the bag from her teacher's head. "Ms. Miller," she cried out. "Oh, my God. . . ."

Ms. Miller opened her mouth and made a painful gasp for air. She began to cough and fell from the chair to the floor.

"Are you okay?" Cordelia asked her.

"Attacked . . . Didn't see . . ." Ms. Miller responded. She was barely able to choke the words out.

As the teacher began to cough once again, Cordelia heard the scratching of chalk on the chalkboard behind her. Turning, she came face-to-face with the writing on the wall.

LISTEN

Buffy was the last to arrive at the library. Willow, Xander, and Giles had already assembled around the large wooden table when the Slayer arrived, her face flushed with excitement of discovery.

"It looked like she'd been there for months," Buffy said once she'd caught her breath. "It's where I found this." She placed the yearbook on the table. "Check it out."

Willow's braided head moved up and down as she quickly scanned the words written in Marcie's yearbook. "Oh my God," she gasped sadly as she read. "'Have a nice summer.' 'Have a nice summer.' 'Have a nice summer.' . . . This girl had no friends at all."

Giles looked at her curiously. The messages seemed nice enough to him. "Once again I teeter at the precipice of the generation gap."

"'Have a nice summer' is what you write when you have nothing to say," Buffy explained.

"It's the kiss of death," Xander seconded.

Buffy looked at her friends suspiciously. "And you guys didn't know Marcie Ross?" she asked.

Xander shook his head. "Never met her. Why?"

Buffy pushed the yearbook toward him. "'Cause you both wrote it too."

Xander searched the page for his signature. There it was, in the bottom left corner of the inside cover. "'Have a nice . . .' Yeesh!" he admitted sheepishly.

"Where am I?" Willow interjected. "Oh. 'Have a *great* summer.'" She smiled hopefully at the others. "See? I cared."

Buffy frowned. "But you don't remember her."

Xander looked helpless. "Well, we probably didn't see her except to sign this book," he remarked in an effort to excuse himself. "This is a big school."

"Xander," Willow interrupted as she grabbed a copy of Marcie's transcript from her pile of missing-persons reports. "We each had four classes with her last year."

Buffy sighed sadly, trying to imagine the loneliness

Marcie must have felt. "So no one noticed her," she mused, "and now she's invisible."

Xander rolled his eyes. "What, she turned invisible because no one noticed her?"

Giles pounded his fist firmly on the wooden table. "Of course!" he exclaimed excitedly. He leaped over toward a bookshelf and yanked out a textbook entitled *Introduction to Quantum Mechanics*. "I've been investigating mystical causes of invisibility when I should have looked to the quantum mechanical—physics."

Buffy shot him a confused look. "I think I speak for everyone here when I say, 'huh?'"

"Reality is shaped, even created, by our perception of it."

Three confused faces stared back at Giles.

"People perceived Marcie as invisible and she became so," the librarian explained in a language his charges could comprehend.

Listening to Giles's explanation, Willow tried frantically to picture Marcie in one of her classes. Marcie was one of those people who faded into the background, even with the teachers. Ms. Miller had never noticed her, preferring to call on Cordelia or other students of higher visibility instead.

Willow didn't realize it, but it was in Ms. Miller's English class that Marcie had first noticed herself disappearing. It was a moment Marcie herself could never forget. She'd tried to answer a question about the heroism of the protagonist. Marcie had been the first to raise her hand, but as usual, Ms. Miller had called someone else. And when Marcie had finally admitted defeat and lowered her hand, she'd noticed with fear and wonder that she could see right through her fingers.

And yet, Marcie recalled wryly, *even that remarkable transformation had occured without anyone else in the class ever knowing it.*

"People perceived the whole Marcie package as invisible, clothes and all?" Xander puzzled aloud. "So you're saying she's not naked."

"It isn't this great power she can control, it's something that was done to her," Buffy reasoned, ignoring yet another of Xander's inappropriately prurient ideas. "That *we* did to her."

"No wonder she's miffed," Willow said.

"But what does she want?" Xander asked, giving a voice to the question they were all thinking.

Buffy turned the pages of the yearbook until she came up with the answer. There was a full-page picture of Cordelia, all smiles and joy. At least that's what it seemed to be. It was hard to tell. Marcie had covered the picture with wild pen scratches and drawn a hideous red crown on Cordy's head.

"Just what we thought," she told Xander. "Cordelia."

As if on cue, the prom queen herself came tearing into the library, a look of sheer panic on her face. "I knew I'd find you here," she told Buffy. She seemed to have no idea that she'd interrupted anything. "Buffy, I, uh, know we've had our differences, you being so weird and all, and hanging out with these—ugh—*total losers* and . . ." Cordelia looked at the expressions on the faces of Buffy and her friends. *Oops. Wrong approach.* "Well, anyway," she continued, changing tactics, "despite all that, I know you share this feeling we have for each other deep down. . . ."

"Nausea?" Willow interrupted.

That was it. "Somebody's after me!" she screamed, somewhat hysterically. "They just tried to kill Ms. Miller! And she was helping me with homework! And Mitch and Harmony! This is all about me! Me! Me!"

Xander laughed. "Wow. For once she's right."

"So why are you coming to me for help?" Buffy asked Cordelia.

Cordelia sighed and bit her perfectly painted lip. "Because you're always around when stuff happens. I know you're strong, and you've got those weapons. I was kind of hoping you're in a gang."

Willow choked back a giggle at the thought.

"Please. . . . I don't know where else to turn," Cordelia begged.

Giles jumped up and offered Cordelia his chair "Please, sit down," he suggested. As Cordelia took a seat, Giles peered at her curiously. "Do you know, I don't recall ever seeing you here before."

Cordelia smiled sweetly. "Oh, no. I have a life," she explained, perfectly deadpan.

Buffy shook her head with a slight air of frustration. "Cordelia, the attacker is an invisible girl."

"Who is really, really angry with you," Xander added. "I can't imagine that, personally, but it takes all kinds, you know?"

Xander's sarcasm went right past Cordelia. "I don't care what it is. Just get rid of it."

"It's not that simple," Buffy told her as she opened

the yearbook to Marcie's picture. "It's a person. This person—do you have any idea why she would be so—"

"God, is she really wearing *Laura Ashley?*" Cordelia asked incredulously, scanning the photo.

"So *homicidal?*" Xander piped in, finishing Buffy's question.

Cordelia shook her head emphatically. "I have no idea at all! I've never seen this girl before in my life."

But while Cordelia may not have remembered Marcie, Marcie certainly remembered her . . . *with a vengeance.*

She was at that very moment stomping around her lair becoming more and more angry. "I'll show them," she muttered. "Idiots. Show them all. They're never gonna forget. Ought to *Kill.* I could *Kill.* I'm right here. I'm coming for you. Right behind you, idiots."

But back at the library Cordelia could hear none of that, and neither could the others. They were listening to Cordelia tell her tale. As she spoke, Giles looked at the frantic May Queen and sighed. This situation had escalated much more quickly than he'd anticipated.

"According to what you've told us about the attack on Ms. Miller we now have two messages from Marcie," he remarked. "'Look' and 'Listen.'"

"Messages we don't understand," Willow moaned.

"I'm not sure we're supposed to . . . yet. Marcie's not quite ready." Buffy began to puzzle things out aloud. "From what she did to Cordelia's picture I'd say she's wigged out on the whole May Queen thing. Maybe she's going to do something about it, but at a time of her choosing."

Willow considered that for a moment. "Stop the coronation tonight," she suggested finally. "Keep you guys out of the Bronze."

Cordelia looked at Willow as though she had four heads. "*Nothing* is keeping me from the Bronze tonight," she declared defiantly.

Xander shook his head in disbelief. "Can we just revel in your fabulous lack of priorities?"

Buffy bit her lip, holding back a laugh. But Cordelia would not be dissuaded. "If I'm not crowned tonight, then Marcie's won! And that's bad," she argued. She glared at Xander's look of disbelief. "She's evil, okay? Way eviler than me."

"Cordelia has a point," Buffy told the others.

Cordelia smiled triumphantly. "Buffy's with me on this."

"Continuing the normal May Queen activities is probably the best way to draw Marcie out," Buffy explained. "We can use Cordelia as bait."

"Great," Cordelia began. *Wait.* "What? Bait?"

But the Avengers had already begun to assemble. "Willow and Xander will help me begin our research anew," Giles told Buffy.

Xander rolled his eyes. "He can just say that and then we have to."

Giles glared at Xander—well, glared in a stiff-upper-lip, English, no-emotion sort of way. It was important that he communicate the importance of this mission. "Unless we can find a way to cure Marcie's invisibility, Buffy will be—"

"A sitting duck," Buffy said matter-of-factly. She was used to it. She turned to Cordelia. "Come on."

"I need to try on my dress," Cordelia told Buffy. Then she gasped. "Am I really bait?"

Buffy rolled her eyes. *Which would you prefer, Cordy: "Bait," or "dead"?*

Cordelia watched as Buffy peered around the corner, checking the hallways for danger. Against all instinct, she was impressed by Buffy's take charge attitude. Way action-hero.

"So how much the creepy is it that this Marcie's been at this for months?" Cordelia mused out loud. "Spying on us, learning our most guarded secrets . . ."

Buffy looked around, trying to sense if Marcie was spying at them right now. There didn't seem to be any sign of her.

"And she turned invisible 'cause she's so unpopular," Cordelia continued. "Bummer for her."

Buffy sighed. Cordelia definitely had her own way of putting things. "That about sums it up," she agreed.

Cordelia stopped for a second and looked earnestly into Buffy's green eyes. "It's awful to feel that lonely," she said simply.

Buffy sneered. "Oh, so you've read about that feeling?"

But Cordelia was serious. "You think I'm never lonely, just 'cause I'm so cute and popular?" she pressed. "I can be surrounded by people and be completely alone. It's not like any of them really know me. I don't even know if they really like me half the time. People just want to be in the popular zone. Sometimes when I talk, everyone's so busy agreeing with me, they don't hear a word I say."

Buffy thought about that for a moment. In a strange way, what Cordelia was saying made sense. Or at least, sort of. "If you feel so alone," Buffy asked, "why do you work so hard to be popular?"

Cordelia tossed her hair and shrugged. "It beats being alone all by yourself."

Buffy choked back a laugh as Cordelia started down the stairs. It was tough to argue with that sort of logic.

"Perhaps we can talk to her, reason with her," Giles suggested as he, Willow, and Xander sat by themselves in the library. "Or possibly grab her," he added.

Willow thought about that for a moment. "There *are* three of us," she said, with just a touch of doubt in her voice.

But Xander was all über-macho man. "Let's go!" he exclaimed.

That's when they heard the soft, woeful sounds of a single flute. Quickly they rushed into the hall of the school, hoping to discover where the melancholy music was coming from.

The boiler room. Quickly, the trio raced downstairs toward the basement. With no fear for his personal safety, Giles entered the dark, hot room. Willow and Xander followed close behind.

"Marcie," the librarian called out. "We know what has happened to you. Can we talk to you?

"We're so sorry we ignored you," Willow added.

But Marcie didn't answer. The only response was the music playing on. It seemed to be coming from the boiler itself. Carefully the trio crept around the boiler, only to discover that Marcie wasn't playing the flute at all. Instead they found a small tape player, broadcasting a cassette of flute music.

"Can you say 'gulp'?" Xander asked nervously as he raced for the door. But before he could even reach the handle, Marcie's maniacal laugh rang through the boiler room. She giggled wildly as the door slammed shut.

Giles and Xander pushed on the door, trying desperately to force it open. But the huge metal door wouldn't budge. It was locked from the outside.

Suddenly they heard a frightening hissing noise. The sound was unmistakable. "Gas!" Giles exclaimed.

Buffy led Cordelia into her makeshift changing room. Despite the imminent danger, she was busy dealing with Cordelia's latest worries.

"If you ever tell anyone I changed in the mop closet . . . ," Cordelia threatened as she watched Buffy check the supply closet for an sign of Marcie.

"Your secret dies with me," Buffy assured her. "Looks okay. But hurry."

Buffy slipped out of the closet and shut the door to give Cordelia some privacy. As Cordelia carefully unbuckled the belt of her pale yellow sundress and prepared to change, the Slayer paced back and forth on the other side of the closed door, wishing she could hurry her along.

"You know, what you were saying before, I understand," Buffy confided to Cordelia through the closed door. "It doesn't matter how popular you are—"

"You were popular?" Cordelia interrupted. "In what alternate universe?"

"In L.A.," Buffy told her. "The point is, I did sort of feel like something was missing. . . ."

"Is that when you became weird and got kicked out of school?"

Buffy sighed, exasperated. "Okay," she said, trying to maintain her calm. "Can we have the heartfelt talk with less talk from you?"

Apparently, Cordelia took what Buffy had said to heart, because there was only the sound of silence coming from the supply closet.

Which is so not Cordy's M.O.

"Cordelia?" Buffy called out.

There was still no answer. Suddenly Buffy heard a loud thump, as though someone had knocked over a bucket or tripped over something. "Cordelia!" Buffy cried out again.

Now Buffy could hear a loud commotion coming from within the closet. There was definitely a struggle going on. Quickly Buffy turned the doorknob. But someone—probably Marcie—had jammed the lock. She rammed her shoulder into the door, hoping to knock it loose, but the door wouldn't budge. Finally Buffy tightened her fist and punched a hole in the door, allowing her to reach in and turn the knob.

Buffy rushed into the closet just in time to see Cordelia's feet dangling wildly from the ceiling. Buffy stretched tall and reached up, trying to grab one of Cordelia's ankles, but Cordy was too high up. Buffy grabbed a pile of boxes and stacked them beneath the hole in the ceiling. She climbed up onto the stack and pulled herself up into a crawl space in the ceiling.

Buffy waited there for a moment, listening. Suddenly she heard a dull thud, followed by the sound of someone dragging something heavy across a wooden floor. She crawled in the direction of the sound. Within a few seconds she found herself back in Marcie's lair. There, in the dim light, she saw Cordelia's limp, unconscious body. Instinctively, Buffy reached for her classmate.

But Marcie was too quick for her. She flung her invisible body directly into Buffy, sending the slayer flying sideways from the nest. Buffy slammed into the ceiling tiles. The tiles caved beneath her weight, sending Buffy crashing into the classroom below.

As Buffy struggled to get her bearings, she could hear Marcie landing on the floor beside her. Although Buffy couldn't see the girl, she *could* see the brown leather bag she was holding in her hands. The bag opened, and, from the corner of her eye, Buffy could see a huge, dripping hypodermic needle floating beside her. The Slayer tried to move out of the way, but it was too late. The needle plunged into her neck. With a small gasp, Buffy went limp.

Giles, Xander, and Willow weren't faring much better in the boiler room. It was obvious that Marcie had snuffed out the pilot light, and now the room was filling up with gas. There was no way to stop the flow of the invisible poisonous fumes. Marcie had made sure to disengage the valve.

Even breaking down the door was out. Giles had made it quite clear that doing so was a bad idea. If the metal door let out a single spark, the entire room would go up in flames.

Already, the fumes were making the trio woozy. "Why is Marcie doing this?" Willow moaned.

"The isolation, the exile she's endured," Giles explained in a voice much slower than his usual. "She has gone mad."

Understatement of the year. "Ya think?" Xander barked at the librarian. He listened to the slow, ominous hissing of leaking gas. *If we don't get out of here soon . . .*

It was a thought Xander couldn't bring himself to finish.

Buffy wasn't sure how much time had passed since she'd fallen onto the band room floor, when she found herself in a strange, dark space, struggling to open her eyes. At first her vision was blurred with the after effects of whatever Marcie had injected into her, but eventually she was able to make out Cordelia's face staring at her. The brunette was sitting a few feet from Buffy, tied to an ornately decorated chair—a throne maybe. She was wearing her new gown and some sort of crown.

It took Buffy a few minutes to realize where she was. Somehow, Marcie had managed to drag the girls over to the Bronze, where Cordelia's May Queen coronation party was all set up. That explained the throne and the tiara, but it didn't explain why Marcie had taken them there.

Buffy struggled to stand, but it was impossible. The invisible girl had managed to tie both girls to their chairs. Mad or not, Marcie was one smart girl. She'd left nothing to chance.

"Buffy? You're awake?" Cordelia asked softly.

"Yeah."

"I can't feel my face."

Buffy looked at her curiously. "What do you mean?"

"My face! It feels numb." Cordelia cried out, the panic in her voice unmistakable. "What is she doing?"

"I don't know," Buffy told her honestly.

Cordelia turned her head slightly and looked straight ahead. Buffy followed the direction of Cordelia's gaze. On the wall, in huge red letters, Marcie had painted a single word.

LEARN

"What does that mean?" Cordelia asked Buffy.

"I don't know," Buffy repeated. There didn't seem to be any other response.

Just then a small cart covered with an old ratty towel appeared at Cordelia's side. It seemed to be rolling by itself—meaning Marcie was nearby. As if to prove that fact, Marcie spoke to the girls. "I'm disappointed," the invisible girl remarked ruefully. "I really hoped you guys would have figured it out by now."

Buffy could hear the growing venom in Marcie's tone. She would have to keep the invisible girl calm; keep her from making things worse than they already were.

"Come on Marcie," Buffy said, her own voice slow and steady. "Why don't you explain it? What are we supposed to learn?"

There was silence. And for a moment Buffy thought

that maybe—just *maybe*—Marcie was going to explain what was going on.

But then Cordelia opened her mouth to speak.

"Yeah, what do you want to teach us?"

The sound of Cordelia's superiority-drenched voice destroyed any possibility of Marcie feeling a sense of comfort and acceptance. "No, you don't get it," she spat. "You're not the student. You're the *lesson*."

That *so* did not sound good. Buffy and Cordelia glanced at each other nervously. Finally Cordelia spoke, her voice taking on a whole new level of hesitance and stress. "What have you done to my face?"

"Your face," Marcie scoffed. "That's what it's all about, isn't it? Your beautiful face. That's what makes you shine just a little brighter than the rest of us. We all want to be noticed. To be remembered. To be seen."

Swiftly the invisible girl whipped the towel from the rolling cart, revealing an impressive array of surgical tools: scalpels, knives, scissors, and hypodermic needles, each more ancient and horrific than the one before.

"What are you doing?" Cordelia asked, her voice rapidly approaching panic level.

Marcie's reply was perfectly calm. "I'm gonna give you a face no one will ever forget. . . ."

The air in the boiler room was dangerously heavy with gas. Giles, Willow, and Xander were now so weak that they couldn't stand. They sat still on the hard cement floor, their bodies slumped over, their breath so pained they could do little more than wheeze.

"I'm thinking we ram the door and take our chances," Xander told the others. He reached over and took a large metal pipe in his hands.

"What're a few sparks between friends?" Willow agreed weakly.

Giles struggled to force his brain to think. "Sparks . . . ," he said slowly, "sparks are caused by metal on metal." Quickly Giles removed his tweed jacket and wrapped it around Xander's metal pipe. The librarian stood and motioned for the others to do the same.

Coughing fiercely, Willow and Xander struggled to their feet. The threesome held the large pipe straight out, like a battering ram, and prepared to break down the door.

"One, two, three," Giles wheezed. The threesome ran towards the door.

Bam!

The door didn't budge.

"Again!" Giles ordered.

Bam!

It was no use. The door was locked tight. Sadly, Willow, Xander, and Giles sagged against the wall, coughing wildly. Each breath was a struggle. The gas was suffocating them.

It wouldn't be long now.

Buffy sat straight in her chair and tried to stay perfectly calm. Despite her near desperation at being held prisoner, she didn't make any attempt to break the ropes that bound her. The last thing she wanted was for Marcie to thinking she was desperate. Buffy had to appear to have the upper hand.

Unfortunately, *Marcie's* hand didn't appear at all—putting the Buffster at a distinct disadvantage.

Buffy wasn't sure what Marcie planned to do with her collection of masochistic medical tools, but she was certain that she had to keep the invisible girl from whatever her plans might be.

"Marcie . . . you can't do this," Buffy said, appealing to the part of the girl that was still human.

Marcie laughed. "What are you gonna do? *Slay* me?" she asked.

So much for not appearing desperate. Time to go into slayer mode. Quickly Buffy struggled against the ropes that held her prisoner. The knots were solid. *Okay, so slaying, pretty much a no-go for right now.*

"Marcie, you know it's wrong," Buffy reminded her.

Slam! Buffy's head whipped to the side as Marcie punched her in the face. The Slayer hadn't seen that coming. *Duh.*

"You should have stayed out of my way," Marcie told Buffy. "You know, I actually thought you might understand my vision. But you're just like them."

Buffy shook her head. She knew what Marcie meant. Cordelia and her gang of Cordettes could be cruel in their exclusivity. It was easy to feel left out, mocked, ridiculed. But no matter how badly Buffy might feel, she could never have done anything like this. Of that, she was certain.

"Please, don't do this," Cordelia begged.

Cordelia's pitiful pleas were all it took for Marcie to reaffirm her own conviction. Suddenly a cold metal scalpel rose up in the air, its blade directed straight at

Cordelia's cheek. Marcie's plan was now clear.

"No!" Cordelia cried out.

"You should be grateful," Marcie mocked. "People who pass you in the street will remember you for the rest of their lives. Children will dream about you. And every one of your friends who comes to the coronation tonight will take the sight of the May Queen to their graves."

As Marcie spoke, Buffy glanced down at the tray. A scalpel rested right on the edge, almost near enough for Buffy to reach. If she could just inch her way toward the tray she could . . .

From the corner of her eye, Cordelia spotted Buffy reaching for the scalpel. If she could just keep Marcie occupied for another minute . . .

"Wait!" Cordelia cried out.

But Marcie had waited long enough. "We really have to get started," she told Cordelia. "The local anesthetic will be wearing off soon, and I don't want you to faint. It's less fun if you're not awake."

Slowly she moved the scalpel closer to Cordelia's perfect cheek.

"You're blacking out on me, guys!" Xander moaned as his body slumped nearer to the floor. In a second he was still. Willow too, was losing her battle for consciousness.

Giles made one last feeble attempt to open the door. He reached over and pressed his weight against it one more time. Miraculously, it opened! The door *opened,* just like that. There, standing alone in the doorway, was

Angel. The vampire opened his dark eyes wide and peered into room, taking in the sight of Willow and Xander near death on the floor. "Come on," he called to Giles as he lifted Willow and carried her to safety. Frantically, Giles shook Willow's lifeless body, trying to get her to breathe, to open her eyes, as Angel went back for Xander.

"What happened?" a semiconscious Xander moaned as Angel placed him on the floor in the basement hall.

"You tell me," Angel replied.

"I'm up, Mom," Willow mumbled incoherently as she struggled to regain consciousness.

Xander blinked and stared at Angel. The vampire always seemed to be around when there was trouble. Angel had just saved them from certain death, but it was still hard for Xander to be grateful. *Sure. Jealous much, Xand?* he asked himself. "What do you want?" he snapped at Angel. *Yeah, I guess I am.*

Angel turned and spoke directly to Giles. "I brought you the *Codex*," he explained, reminding Giles of the book they had discussed earlier. "I came in through the basement, smelled the gas."

The gas! "We've still got to turn it off," Giles recalled. "It could blow the building."

Angel nodded and headed for the door. "I'll do it. It's not like I need the oxygen," he assured him.

Buffy's hand edged nearer and nearer to the blade at the side of the cart. Slowly she slipped it into her palm and closed her fist, taking care not to cut herself in the process. Marcie didn't seem to notice; she was too focused on Cordelia's face.

"Let me see," the invisible girl mused. "I think we should start with your smile. I think it should be wider."

"Marcie, listen," Cordelia pleaded. "You think I don't understand what you're going through, but I do."

"I'll bet you know how I feel," Marcie laughed, mocking her. "I'll bet you can be with all your friends and feel so alone because they don't really know you." She laughed again as the surprise registered in Cordelia's eyes. "You're a typical self-involved spoiled little brat. You think you can charm your way out of this. Isn't that what you think?" And with that Marcie drew her hand wildly across Cordelia's face. The scalpel left it's mark: a straight red gash across the May Queen's cheek. Cordelia cried out, her eyes filling with tears.

Just then Buffy sliced the last of the ropes from around her leg. She was free. Quickly the Slayer kicked the cart away. It stopped suddenly, hitting an invisible object with a thud. Marcie's cry of pain let Buffy know the cart had hit its mark.

"Oh, God, get me out of here!" Cordelia screamed. She squirmed wildly in her chair as Buffy bent down to cut her free.

"Just hold still," Buffy ordered as she sliced at the ropes. But before Buffy could free Cordelia, she felt a heavy boot kick her right in the stomach. The force literally sent her flying across the room. Quickly Buffy rose to her knees, but before she could stand, an invisible kick to her face forced her to fall backward.

Okay, you know what, Marcie? For a while there, I felt your pain. I truly did. Now you're gonna feel mine. Big time.

"You know, I really felt bad for you. You've suffered," Buffy shouted into the empty space. "But there's one thing I didn't factor into all this. You're a thundering loony!" She turned and swung at the air with all her might . . . and hit nothing.

"Hey, moron," Marcie taunted. "I'm invisible." *Wham!* She gave Buffy another left hook to the face. Buffy swung back . . . and missed again.

Buffy's mind raced. *Look. Listen. Learn.* What was it Giles had said as they sat together outside the school, watching Xander and Willow head off for Chinese food? Oh, yeah. Something about her listening to people for a change. That was the answer.

Cordelia whimpered.

"Cordelia, shut up!" Buffy ordered.

"Okay." Cordelia's voice was small now, like a frightened, lost child. But Buffy couldn't deal with Cordelia just now. She had to locate Marcie. The Slayer stood still in the center of the room. *Looking, not so helpful.* Suddenly the sounds around her grew louder, as though they were amplified in her ears. So she *listened.* Just listened. Marcie's rapid breathing grew closer and closer. Her footsteps forced the floorboards to creak ever so slightly and then . . .

Wham! Buffy turned around and punched at the air with all her might. Her fist connected with some part of Marcy's body with a force hard enough to send the invisible girl flying across the room and into a red velvet curtain. The curtain covered Marcy's invisible body, allowing Buffy to discern where she stood. "I see you," the Slayer declared. With one final punch, she knocked Marcie to the ground.

Buffy stood over the invisible girl for a moment, ready if she should rise again. But before either girl could move, two men in black—the same men who had been loitering in the bushes of the quad during Cordelia's acceptance speech—burst into the Bronze.

"Everybody stay where you are!" The shorter of the two men announced.

"We'll take it from here," his partner assured Buffy.

Um, huh? "Take it from where?" Buffy asked.

One of the men flashed his badge quickly. "I'm Agent Doyle. This is Agent Manetti. We're here for the girl."

Buffy rolled her eyes. "Where were you ten minutes ago when she was playing surgeon?"

"We came as fast as we could," Agent Doyle assured her. "We'll take care of it from here on." He reached down and helped Marcie to her feet.

Marcie walked slowly toward the door, the two agents holding her by the arms. The only way Buffy could tell that Marcie was there was by the red curtain that was still wrapped around her body. A sudden wave of pity came over Buffy. "You can cure her?" she asked hopefully.

"We can . . . rehabilitate her," Agent Doyle replied, in a decidedly noncommittal voice.

"In time, she'll learn to be a useful member of society again," Agent Manetti added.

Buffy eyed the two men suspiciously. "This isn't the first time this has happened is it?" she demanded finally. "This has happened at other schools."

"We're not at liberty to discuss that," Agent Manetti replied.

"It would be best for you to forget this whole incident," Agent Doyle assured Buffy.

"Do you guys know that you're very creepy?" Buffy said.

Agent Doyle had no response to that. "Thank you for your help," he murmured as he and Agent Manetti led Marcie from the Bronze.

Buffy stood and watched pensively as they left. The agents had promised to help Marcie, to rehabilitate her. But Buffy couldn't imagine where the agents could take her. Where in the world could an invisible, homicidal girl learn to fit in?

Buffy's thoughts were broken by the sound of Cordelia's uncharacteristically meek voice. "Can I get untied now?" she asked.

A full day after Cordelia's coronation, Buffy was still obsessing over what had happened to Marcie. This confrontation had really gotten to her. Maybe it was because Marcie wasn't a vampire or a monster. She was a girl—a girl who had been turned into a killer by the people around her.

"I just can't believe how twisted Marcie got," she pondered out loud as she walked down the halls of Sunnydale High with Willow, Xander, and Giles. "How did you guys get out of the boiler room?"

Willow opened her mouth to speak, but a look from Giles forced her to stop before the words left her mouth. "Janitor," Giles said quickly. "Found us and shut off the valve."

"We were lucky," Willow added.

"I'll say," Buffy agreed.

Just then Cordelia approached the foursome. Other than a small cut on her cheek, she bore no mark of the horrors of the night before. In fact, she seemed happier than ever.

"Hey," Buffy greeted her.

"Hi. Look, I didn't get a chance to say anything yesterday, with the coronation and everything, but . . ." She stopped and took a breath. Words like these didn't always come easily to Cordelia. "I guess I want to thank you," she said finally. "All of you."

Xander broke the silence. "It's funny, 'cause you *look* like Cordelia," he joked.

"You really helped me out, and you didn't have to, so thanks," Cordelia continued.

"That's okay," Buffy assured her.

Willow smiled. "Listen, we're just going to grab some lunch. If you wanted—"

Before Willow could continue her invitation, Mitch came wandering down the hall with a few of Cordelia's friends in tow. The group of popular kids stopped just short of Buffy and her friends.

"Whoa!" Mitch exclaimed, making no attempt to hide the surprise—make that *disgust*—in his voice. "You're not hanging with these losers are you?"

Cordelia fidgeted nervously for a second. But it didn't take long for her natural sense of self-preservation to return. "Are you kidding?" she laughed. "I was just being charitable, trying to help them with their fashion problems." She took Mitch's arm and walked off without even so much as glancing back. "You really think I felt like joining that social leper colony?" she asked Mitch. "Please."

Xander watched Cordelia and her fans disappear into the distance. "Boy, where's an invisible girl when you need one?"

Marcie walked slowly down the school hallway flanked on either side by Agents Doyle and Manetti. Despite the fact that the two men in black couldn't actually see her, Marcie knew better than to bolt. *Besides, things at this school couldn't be worse than they'd been at Sunnydale, right?*

Marcie was more than a little disappointed to discover that the new school looked a lot like Sunnydale High—lockers lining the walls, and classroom doors swinging closed just as the bell rang, signaling that class had begun. The only difference was that the hallways appeared to be empty.

"We think you'll be happy here," Agent Doyle assured her.

"You should fit right in," Agent Manetti added.

They stopped by a classroom. The door opened, as if by itself. The room appeared empty, except for a single teacher who stood in the front of the room.

But the room wasn't empty at all. It was filled with students just like Marcie.

"Welcome Marcie. Please sit down." The teacher smiled as she turned toward the rest of her class. "Okay class, please turn to page fifty-four in your texts."

Instantly the textbooks opened. To an outsider, it appeared that the books were moving on their own. But Marcie knew better. She glanced at the chapter subhead: *Assassination and Infiltration.*

"Cool," she muttered to herself.

"Some Assembly Required"

Cordelia frowned as she took a sip of her mocha java. *Not enough mocha.* Wasn't that always the problem? Oh, well. There wasn't much she could do about it, since the coffee bar at the Bronze was completely packed, and she'd never be able to get the attention of that attendant again. Slowly she got up and wandered over toward the table where Harmony and some of the others were already sitting. They'd saved her a spot at the head of the table. *Duh.* At least *some* things at the Bronze were exactly as they should be tonight.

As she headed across the dance floor, Cordelia caught a glimpse of Buffy, Xander, and Willow walking through the door of the club. She smiled brightly and started to wave—then stopped herself, reaching up to smooth her hair instead, as she noticed Harmony and the other Cordettes staring at her with surprise. Cordelia couldn't blame them, actually. It must look odd, Cordelia Chase greeting the library-nerd patrol. After all, Harmony and the others had no idea what Cordelia, Buffy, Willow, and Xander had all been through together recently.

Evidently, Buffy was like some kind of superhero or something. All of those weird, creepy incidents that seemed to take place around her? Yeah, that was on purpose. And somehow Cordelia had been sucked up into the Slayer's circle.

Cordelia'd been ordered not to tell anyone about Buffy being the Slayer. Xander had explained to her that no one could know. It would destroy everything.

Cordelia smiled a bit as she thought of Xander. *With a little work, he could be* . . . Cordelia stopped herself right there. *No. Once a nerd, always a nerd.*

At least that's what Cordelia had always believed. But so much had happened between the last school year and now. Not that horrible summer vacation in Tuscany. (Too much art, not enough beach!) All that weird stuff with the vampires and the Master and all that. Cordelia had been right there in the library when Buffy had slayed the Master, the most powerful of vampires—the one who could have opened the Hellmouth and released the Old Ones into Sunnydale, had Buffy not been able to stop him.

Cordelia had seen the whole battle. There had been vampires everywhere—she'd even had to bite one of them to get him off of her (and no amount of Listerine strips would ever get that taste out of her mouth!), until Buffy had managed to flip the Master through the glass skylight in the library. He was impaled on a sharp piece of wood when he landed. *Bam. Straight through the heart*.

But the war between Slayer and Master hadn't ended there. Oh sure, Sunnydale was all sweetness and light over the summer while Buffy was in L.A. with her dad, but as soon as Buffy returned to school, trouble came back too. Trouble always followed Buffy.

Unfortunately, these days trouble seemed to follow Cordelia, too. Or at least she always seemed to be in the wrong place at the right time. Like the fact that she'd been in the room when the Master had been slain. That was a really bad spot to be in, because when the Master's followers decided to dig up his bones and bring him back to life, for the ritual they'd needed those *closest* to him when he died. That meant they needed Cordelia (and Willow and that über-peppy computer teacher Ms. Calendar too, of course, but they seemed to be used to this sort of thing). So once again, Cordelia's life had been in danger—until Buffy had come to the rescue and gotten rid of all those horrible vampires.

The worst part of the whole ordeal—other than indelible stains on her clothes, of course—was that Cordelia had a feeling the memories of those two nights were going to stay with her forever. She'd never forget the taste of that vampire's hand in her mouth or the fear she felt when she thought one of the Master's followers was going to slit her throat.

And who could forget Buffy's weird reaction to killing the Master? The girl had played some heavy mind games on her friends—freezing out Angel while turning the heat up with Xander during a hormone-heavy slow dance at the Bronze. Pure bad girl.

For some reason, watching Buffy get Xander all hot and bothered—and then leaving him high and dry—really pissed Cordelia off. In fact she'd told Buffy to get past the thing with the Master and stop being a total jerk. Otherwise Buffy was going to lose the few loser friends she had.

Cordy wasn't sure why she'd snapped at Buffy's vixen act with Xander. Or why she'd cared whether Buffy's friends dumped her or not. But she *had* cared. A lot.

Still, those thoughts—serious thoughts no less— would have to remain private to the people who knew Cordelia best. She could never tell her friends about any of it. Which made her wonder, not for the first time: Did her so-called friends really know her at all?

With all the fear and panic that came with her vampire run-ins, Cordelia had also felt more brave and alive than she'd ever been before. In fact Cordelia had never felt more powerful than when she'd been with Buffy and the other members of the Scooby Squad.

Suddenly a dark figure by the doorway caught Cordelia's eye. His hair was short and thick—the kind you could imagine running your hands through. He was well-built, too. Cordelia could see that even though his muscles were obscured by his dark jacket. This guy was definitely hot, even if he was a little bit older than Cordelia's usual fantasy men.

He was just standing there, watching as Buffy

danced with her friends. He didn't go over to Buffy or even try to catch her eye. All he did was stare.

Cordelia sighed as she recognized him as Angel, the majorly hot—if majorly strange—guy who always seemed to be hanging around Buffy. Cordelia didn't know much about him, except that he was adorable, mysterious, and for some reason seemed far more obsessed with Buffy Summers than with her. Add that to the list of odd things occurring in Sunnydale.

Everything was so confusing these days. What Cordelia needed right now was the comfort of the familiar as she straightened things out. So she strolled across the dance floor and over toward Harmony and the others. There would be no demons facing Cordelia at that table—except, possibly, her own.

Buffy sat alone atop a gravestone in the cemetery . . . waiting. She'd been there most of the night, and now she was getting annoyed. She had an appointment—of sorts—with the newly deceased, soon to be undead, Stephan Korshak. But the newbie was late in rising.

Buffy reached into her pocket and pulled out a plastic yo-yo. She had to pass the time somehow. But the Slayer didn't lose her edge as she pulled the toy up and down; in her other hand she held a large wooden stake. "Come on, Stephan, rise and shine," Buffy urged the corpse as she practiced her walk-the-dog. "Some of us have a ton of trig homework waiting."

"Hey!" A deep, smooth voice came from behind, catching Buffy completely off guard. The Slayer spun around, startled by the sound.

"Ack!" she exclaimed.

Angel smiled slightly at her surprise. "Is this a bad time?" he asked.

Buffy leaped off the headstone and tried to regain her bearings. "Are you crazy?" she spat back. "You don't just sneak up on people in a graveyard. You . . . stomp . . . or yodel."

Angel shrugged off her anger. "I heard you were on the hunt."

Buffy nodded slowly. "Supposed to be," she admitted. Then she glanced over at Stephan's grave once again. "Lazy bones here doesn't want to come out and play."

Angel's eyes darted over toward the headstone. He noted the recent date of death carved into the gray rock. "When you first wake up, it's a little disorienting. He'll show."

Buffy looked into Angel's dark eyes. It would be so easy to forget who he was, *what* he was. When not in vamp-face he appeared so human, until he mentioned things like waking up from the dead. "It's weird to think of you going through that," she told him softly.

"It's weird to go through." Angel looked around the cemetery as though he were searching for someone else. "So . . . uh . . . you're here alone?" he asked her finally.

"Yeah. Why?"

Angel looked away. "I just thought you'd have somebody with you . . . Xander or someone."

Buffy seemed confused. "Xander?"

Angel looked slightly flustered. "Or someone."

Buffy smiled at Angel's obvious discomfort with this whole line of conversation. "No. Are you jealous?"

Angel stood a little taller and puffed his chest out. "Of Xander? Please. He's just a kid."

Buffy had to choke back a laugh. Men—even 241-year-old vampire men—could be such children. "Is it 'cause I danced with him?" she teased.

"'Danced with' is a pretty loose term," Angel shot back, unable to control his emotions any longer. "'Mated with' might be a little closer."

Low blow. "You think you're getting a little unfair?" she demanded. "One little dance, and you know I just did it to make you crazy, which by the way"—she eyed him triumphantly—"behold my success."

"I am not jealous!"

"Oh, you're not jealous." Buffy countered. "What? Vampires don't get jealous?"

"See, whenever we fight, you always bring up the vampire thing."

"I didn't come here to fight," Buffy assured him.

Blam. She was knocked to the ground. *Hello, Stephan Korshak.*

"Oh, right . . . I did," Buffy reminded herself as she threw the vampire from her body and stood. Quickly, Buffy glanced at her hand. She was still holding the yo-yo, but that wouldn't do her much good now. "Where's my stake?"

There was no time to look for her stake now. Stephan was on the move. He'd grabbed a nearby shovel and was about to whack Buffy in the skull.

But before the vampire could make his move, Angel charged at him. Stephan slammed the older vampire in the head. Instinctively Buffy moved toward Stephan. Once again, Stephan raised the shovel and swung at Buffy. But this time she was ready for him. She raised her arm high and with a single motion cracked the wooden handle in half, leaving a pointy, ragged edge. Presto, stake-o. Quickly she wrestled the shovel from Stephan's hands and shoved it into his heart. Instantly the vampire dissolved into dust.

Buffy grinned triumphantly. *Score one more for the Slayer.*

But apparently Buffy's battles weren't over. She looked over at Angel, who was currently rubbing the part of his head that had made contact with Stephan's shovel. He still looked angry, and Buffy had a feeling it wasn't at Stephan.

"And what do you mean 'he's just a kid?'" Buffy demanded, returning to their argument before Angel could. *The best defense is a good offense.* "Does that mean I'm just a kid too?"

Angel opened his mouth to speak, but then thought better of it. He shook his head sadly. "Look, obviously I made a mistake coming here tonight." He turned and walked away.

Buffy watched him for a moment and then hurried to catch up. "Oh, no you don't," she insisted as she worked to fall in step. "You can't just turn and walk away. It takes more than that to get rid of me."

Angel turned around as Buffy's voice dropped.

But the Slayer was nowhere to be seen. He looked down by his feet. There, six feet below, in an empty silk-upholstered coffin, lay the Slayer. "You okay?" he asked, barely choking back his amusement.

Buffy sat up stiffly. "I wish people wouldn't leave open graves lying around like this." She raised her hand to Angel, asking for help out of the grave, but his attention had already turned elsewhere.

"So, another vampire has risen tonight," he mused as he scanned the cemetery grounds.

Buffy shook her head soberly. "I don't think so." She felt around at the satin lining in the newly buried coffin and shivered a little. This was extremely creepy. "Whoever was buried here didn't rise from this grave." Using all her might, she pulled herself out of the hole and raced over toward two shallow depressions in the grass. She bent down and picked up a white woman's formal shoe and stared pointedly at Angel. "She was *dragged* from it."

Early the next morning, Rupert Giles sat with his back to the open library door. He had no idea that he was being observed as he nervously fidgeted, gestured, waved his arms in the air, and asked a wooden library chair for a date.

Or at least that's what it appeared he was doing to the two unnoticed onlookers.

"So, what I'm proposing . . . and I don't mean to appear indecorous . . . is a social engagement . . . a date if you will. If you're amenable . . ." He stopped himself and sighed. "Idiot!" he scolded himself.

"Boy, I guess we never realized how much you liked that chair," came a teasing voice from the doorway.

Giles jumped back, startled, to find Buffy and Xander gazing at him with amusement.

"Oh, I, uh . . . ," Giles muttered nervously. "I was just working on . . ."

"Your pick up lines?" Buffy asked him.

Busted.

Giles blushed fiercely. "In a manner of speaking, yes."

"Then if you don't mind a little Gene and Roger," she continued, "I would leave off the 'idiot' part. Being called an idiot tends to take a person *out* of the dating mood."

"Actually, it kind of turns me on," Xander interjected.

Buffy stared at Xander curiously. "I fear you." Then, turning her attention to the clearly flustered librarian, she added, "You might also want to avoid words like 'amenable' and 'indecorous.' Speak English, not whatever they speak in . . ."

"England?" Giles asked.

"Yeah," Buffy agreed. "Just say, 'Hey, I got a thing, maybe you're feeling a thing, and there could be a thing."

Giles frowned. "Well, thank you, Cyrano."

"I'm not done," Buffy assured him. "Then you say, 'How do you feel about Mexican?'"

"About Mexicans?" Giles was completely confused now.

"Mexican *food,*" Buffy explained, unable to hide her amazement with just how clueless Giles really was. "You take her for food . . . for which you then pay."

"Oh, right."

Xander looked from the librarian to the chair he was speaking to. "So, this 'chair' woman, we are talking Ms. Calendar, right?"

Giles sighed. These American teenagers never missed a thing. "What makes you ask that?" he asked quickly.

Xander smiled. He loved being the one who figured things out—not that it happened all that often. "Simple deduction," he explained. "Ms. Calendar is reasonably dollsome, especially for someone in your age bracket; she already knows you're a school librarian, so you don't have to worry about how to break that embarrassing news to her. . . ."

"And she's the only woman we've ever actually seen speaking to you," Buffy interrupted. "Add it all up, it spells 'duh'."

Xander gave Giles a very fatherly look. "Now, is it time for us to talk about the facts of life?" he teased.

"You know, I am suddenly deciding that this is none of your business," Giles told Xander.

But Xander would not be put off. "'Cause you know," he continued, "that whole stork thing is a smoke screen."

Giles knew he had no choice but to change the subject. He turned to Buffy and asked pointedly, "So, how did things go last night? Did Mr. Korshack show up on schedule?"

"More or less. Angel and I took care of him," the Slayer assured him.

"Angel." Xander snorted with disgust.

Buffy ignored him. "There's something else, though. I found an empty grave."

That was all it took to add some real animation to Giles's otherwise prim and proper face. "Grave robbing," he mused. "Well, that's new. Interesting."

Buffy grimaced. "I know that you meant to say 'gross' and 'disturbing.'"

"Yes, of course," Giles agreed sheepishly. "Terrible thing. Must put a stop to it." He paused for moment, fighting back the smile of excitement that was creeping back onto his face. Then he added a quick "Dammit" for effect.

"So why does someone dig up graves?" Xander asked.

Giles thought about that for a moment, but no immediate answers came to mind. "I'll collate some theories," he said finally. "Might help to know who the body belonged to."

"Meredith Todd," Buffy told him. She turned to Xander. "Ring a bell?"

Xander shook his head. The name meant nothing to him.

"She died recently," Buffy prodded, "and she was our age."

Xander thought for a while but could come up with nothing. "Drawing a blank," he admitted finally.

"Well, why don't we ask Willow to fire up this thing"—Giles pointed at a library computer, taking care not to actually touch the machine. Giles feared computers more than just about anything. Which, considering he was a watcher, said a lot—"and track Meredith down."

Buffy nodded. Then she wondered just where Willow had gotten to, anyhow. Buffy hadn't seen her in quite a while.

At that very moment Willow was standing in line in the school lounge, clipboard in hand. It was time to sign up for Sunnydale High's annual science fair, and Willow was very excited. She had a terrific project in mind—one that could finally win her first prize.

As Willow printed her name at the top of her entry form, a flash bulb went off nearby. "Look at those legs," a student named Eric remarked, breathing heavily as he advanced the film in his camera.

Willow turned and scowled at Eric. She had little patience for the aggressive dark haired boy. He was the kind of kid that gave science nerds everywhere a bad name.

Just then a slightly taller boy with light hair and a complex look in his eyes walked over toward Willow. "Eric, knock it off," Chris Epps told his friend.

Willow smiled and shyly glanced over Chris's shoulder to see what he was writing on his clipboard. Chris looked up suddenly, surprised to see Willow so engrossed in his entry blank.

"Hey, Chris," Willow said, trying to sound casual. "I was just wondering what you're going to do this year."

Chris smiled awkwardly. "Why?"

"Well, every year, you win and I place second," Willow explained. "I just thought I'd see what I was up against."

Chris smiled at Willow, and suddenly he didn't seem shy or unbelievably brainy—both of which he most certainly was. He just seemed like a typical guy. "You know what the key is?" he confided. Willow shook her head. "If Dr. Clark doesn't understand your experiment, he gives it higher marks so it looks like he understands your experiment." Chris glanced over at Willow's entry sheet and read the name of her science project aloud. "'Effects of Subviolet Light Spectrum Deprivation on the Development of Fruit Flies.'" He shot Willow a congratulatory smile. "That should do the trick."

Willow grinned. She loved everything about the science fair. Even consistently losing to Chris. At least that provided her with a challenge.

Cordelia, however, did not share Willow's enthusiasm. In fact she was downright unpleasant as she filled out her entry form. "Okay, I'm doing this under protest," she announced to no one in particular. "It's not fair that they're making participation in this year's science fair mandatory. I don't think anyone should have to do anything educational at school if they don't want to."

Willow glanced over Cordelia's shoulder and read the cheerleader's project name. "'The Tomato: Fruit or Vegetable?'" Willow rolled her eyes. "I want something I can finish in a weekend, okay?" she told Willow. Cordelia sighed. *I mean, really.*

Cordelia blinked as a flash bulb went off in her eyes. "Stop it!" she ordered Eric. "What do you think you're doing?" The prom queen pointed up toward the ceiling on the school lounge. "We're under fluorescent lights, for God's sake!"

Eric smiled slyly, which only served to make him look sleazier and considerably more pathetic. "Come on. The camera loves you."

"I thought you yearbook nerds didn't come out of hibernation till the spring," Cordelia suggested.

Eric gave her an almost obscene grin. "It's for my private collection."

Chris walked over toward his friend. "Will you quit it?" he insisted.

Eric gave his answer in the form of yet another flash as he turned toward the door and took a picture of Buffy Summers, who was just entering the room.

"Coming through," Buffy said, as she literally pushed Eric aside to get to her friend. "Hey, Willow. Sorry to interrupt, but . . . it's the Bat Signal."

"Sure, okay," Willow replied. She turned and smiled gratefully toward Chris. "See you. Thanks for the tip."

Cordelia lingered a moment as Buffy and Willow wandered off. Spending too much time near those two definitely could injure her rep. But when she saw Eric leering once again in her direction, Cordelia decided it was worth the risk. Quickly she scurried off after the two girls.

"Cordelia is so fine," Eric purred with a malevolent grin. "You know she'd be just perfect for us."

Chris stared sternly at his friend, his eyes broadcasting a not-so-subtle warning. "Don't be an idiot," he declared. "She's alive."

• • •

Willow sat down in front of one of the library computers and typed in her password. "This shouldn't take long," she assured Buffy, Xander, and Giles. "I'm probably the only girl in school who has the coroner's office bookmarked as a favorite place."

Before Willow could even access the Web site, Cordelia came blasting through the library doors. "Hi." She greeted the Scooby Squad, trying to sound as friendly as she could. "Sorry to interrupt your little undead playgroup, but I need to ask Willow if she'll help me with my science fair project."

"It's a fruit," Willow said, without looking away from her screen.

"I would ask Chris for help, but"—Cordelia clasped her hand to her mouth, becoming teary—"it would bring back too many memories of Daryl."

Buffy was about to ask, "Daryl who?" but she was interrupted by Willow's enthusiastic shout of "I found it."

Buffy and Xander gathered around the computer screen, leaving Cordelia off to the side by herself. "According to this, Meredith Todd died in a car accident last week."

Meredith who? "Of course I've learned to deal with my pain . . . ," Cordelia continued mournfully.

Buffy was obviously focused elsewhere. "And how was her neck?" she asked Willow.

"Fine . . . except for being broken," Willow replied.

Right. But back to me. "Hello?" Cordelia interrupted. "Can we deal with my pain please?"

Xander rolled his eyes. "There, there," he replied in

a flat voice, patting her shoulder apathetically. He turned back toward Willow.

"It says Meredith and two other girls in the car were killed instantly. They were all on the pep squad at Fondren High, on the way to a game."

"You know what this means," Buffy began.

"That Fondren might actually beat Sunnydale in the crosstown body count competition this year?" Xander joked.

"It means she wasn't killed by vampires," Buffy informed him. "So somebody did dig up her corpse."

Cordelia wrinkled her nose with a look of absolute disgust. "Eew! Why is it that every conversation you have has the word 'corpse' in it?"

Buffy and her friends paid Cordelia no mind. "So okay, we've got a body snatcher," Xander thought aloud. "What does that mean?"

Giles held up an old, musty book. "Here's what I've come up with: Demons who eat the flesh of the dead to absorb their souls. Or it could be a voodoo practitioner."

"You mean making a zombie?" Willow interrupted.

"More likely zomb*ies*," Giles explained. "For most traditional purposes, a voodoo priest would require more than one."

Buffy considered that for a moment. "So we should see if the other girls from this accident are AWOL too," she suggested. "Might help figure out what this creep has in mind if we know whether he's dealing in volume."

Xander nodded. "So we dig up some graves tonight?"

"Oh, wow!" Willow piped in excitedly. "A field trip." She turned to Buffy. "Are you gonna call Angel?"

Buffy frowned and grew quiet. "I don't think so."

Xander couldn't hide his smile. "Yeah? Why bother him?"

"We've been sort of . . . never mind. As far as Angel knows, I'm taking the night off, okay?"

Xander had no problem with that. "So, we're all set then," he agreed. "Say nine-ish. B.Y.O. shovel."

"I'll pack some food. Who likes those little powdered donuts?" Willow asked. Xander's hand shot up. Will smiled and looked over across the table. "Cordelia?"

Cordelia's eyes were large with amazement. *Donuts? Dead people?* Cordelia didn't think so. "Darn, I have cheerleader practice tonight," she told the others quickly. "Boy, I wish I'd known you were gonna be digging up dead people sooner; I would have canceled."

Xander shrugged. "All right," he told Cordelia, "but if you run into the army of zombies, could you page us before they eat your flesh?"

He's kidding. He's definitely, seriously kidding. Cordelia turned and hurried out of the library.

Giles looked sternly at Xander. "Xander, zombies don't eat the flesh of the living," he explained.

Xander laughed. "Yeah, I knew that. But did you see that look on her face?"

• • •

That night, the Scooby Squad met at the grave of Cathy Ryan, a seventeen-year-old who had died in the same car as Meredith Todd. Giles and Xander got straight to work digging up her grave, while Willow and Buffy sat propped up against a nearby headstone munching on powdered donuts and sipping hot coffee.

"He was getting all jealous and he wouldn't even admit it," Buffy told her best girlfriend, remembering Angel's behavior of the previous night.

"Jealous of what?" Willow asked.

Buffy shook her head in disbelief. "Of Xander."

That seemed perfectly plausible to Willow. "'Cause you did that sexy dance with him?"

Buffy looked at the ground, sheepishly. "Am I ever gonna live that down?"

"Nope," Willow replied blithely.

Buffy noted the teasing tone in Willow's voice, but she wasn't playing. "Anyway, he's being totally irrational."

Willow shrugged. "Love makes you do the wacky."

"That's the truth."

Just then, Xander looked up from the ever-increasing hole in Cathy Ryan's grave. "You know, this might go faster if you fems picked up a shovel too."

"Sorry," Buffy replied, laughing. "But I'm an old-fashioned girl. I was raised to believe the men dig up the corpses and the women have the babies." Completely ignoring Xander's look of annoyance, she turned her attention back to Willow. "Speaking of the wacky, what was Cordelia's whole riff about painful memories? Who's Daryl?"

"Daryl Epps," Willow explained. "Chris's older brother. He was a big football star. All-state two years ago. A running . . ." Willow thought a minute, trying to recall the name of the position Daryl had played. "A running . . . someone that runs and catches."

Buffy grinned. "Was he a *studly*?"

Willow's eyes opened wide, remembering. "Big time. All the girls were crazy for him."

"And he broke Cordy's heart." Buffy paused for a moment. "Thus possibly proving its existence," she added wryly.

"He died," Willow said quietly. "Rock climbing or something. He fell."

"Oh, man. That's lousy. Poor Chris."

Willow nodded. "Ever since then, he's been real . . . quiet. Kind of in his own world. And I hear his mother doesn't even leave the house anymore."

Buffy nodded. But before she could say anything, the girls heard a loud thunk coming from the open grave.

"I think we're there," Giles called up at them.

Buffy and Willow peered over the edge of the grave as Giles and Xander wiped the last bits of dirt away from Cathy's coffin.

"By the way, are we hoping to find a body or no body?" Willow asked.

"Call me an optimist, but I'm hoping to find a fortune in gold doubloons," Xander gibed.

Buffy carefully considered Willow's question. "Well, body could mean flesh-eating demon," she thought aloud. "No body points more toward the army-of-zombies thing. Take your pick, really."

Xander looked down at the lid of the coffin.

"Go ahead," Giles told him.

"You're closer," Xander disagreed.

Buffy rolled her eyes. "Pathetic much? Move over,"

she ordered as she dropped down into the grave and reached for the latch that opened the coffin.

Cordelia, meanwhile, was busy with her own problems. The cheering squad was missing something—its pep and enthusiasm. As she headed out to the parking lot, she explained the importance of this issue with two other members of the squad. "Guys," she complained, "if we don't have this down by tomorrow then no one will be led by our cheers. Practice."

After assuring Cordelia that they'd do better tomorrow, the two cheerleaders got into their car and drove off, leaving Cordelia alone in the poorly lit parking lot.

At first she didn't sense anything out of the ordinary. But before long a feeling of total creepiness seemed to come over her. Someone was watching her as she walked in the darkness, Cordelia was sure of it. Her ability to sense others even when she couldn't see them had improved immensely in recent months—probably in part due to her sophomore year run-in with that creepy invisible Marcie. And now Cordelia was absolutely sure that she was not alone. "Hello?" she called out weakly across the lot.

But there was no answer. Quickly Cordelia fumbled through her purse for her keys, quickening her pace toward her car. There was no sound at all in the parking lot, other than the quiet tapping of Cordelia's white cheerleading sneakers against the pavement. "Xander Harris," she called out into the dark quiet, "if this is your idea of a joke . . ."

But there was no reply.

As soon as Cordelia reached her car she jammed

the keys into the lock and frantically tried to open the door, but she had lost control of her fumbling fingers. The keys fell to the ground and skittered under the car. Quickly Cordelia bent down to retrieve them. As she looked beneath the car, Cordelia's eyes focused on a pair of black shoes on the other side. She was freaked— *frozen with panic*. She couldn't move, even as she saw the long, dark, shadow begin to come around the car and toward her. *Time to move*. Quickly Cordelia dashed across the parking lot, searching for a good hiding spot—which she found, unfortunately, in the form of the cafeteria dumpster. Still, this was no time to be grossed out by some leftover food slop and dirty napkins.

Cordy was silent, crouched there in the dark with the trash, for what seemed like forever. Finally, slowly, tentatively, Cordelia finally pulled her head out from under the car. She looked up, clutched her chest, and screamed—until she realized that she was staring right into Angel's deep brown eyes.

"Cordelia," he said quietly, looking around the dark empty parking lot. "This is the last place I expected you to hang out."

"Oh, god . . . oh, god," Cordelia huffed as she struggled to come to herself. "It's you. Why were you following me?"

"I wasn't sure it was you at first. I'm looking for Buffy."

Cordelia couldn't hide her slight disappointment. "Buffy?" she asked. "Well she's—big shock—at the graveyard."

A look of surprise and disappointment came over Angel's face. "She said she'd be home," he thought aloud.

Cordelia shrugged. "Oh, she lied. Isn't she a rascal?"

The look of betrayal on Angel's face was unmistakable. Cordelia had had a lot of experience with guys. She knew this was her moment. *Grab him while he's vulnerable.* She flashed Angel one of her brightest smiles. "But luck is on your side," she told him. "It just so happens my night's free." Coyly she reached out her hand for Angel to help her out of the dumpster. Angel reluctantly took her small hand in his and gave her a tug. Cordelia struggled to stand, but realized that her short yellow and blue cheering skirt was caught on something under the car. "Hold on. My skirt is caught," she explained as she reached behind herself and tried to loosen the uniform. As her skirt came free, Cordelia stood straight and smiled. "There, that's—"

But Cordelia never finished her sentence. The rest of her words were swallowed by her screams as she discovered that her skirt had been held captive by a human hand . . . that was no longer attached to any body.

The Scooby Squad entered the school library, shovels in hand. They were so focused on the information they'd just gathered at the graveyard, they didn't seem to notice that the lights in the room were on, although the school had been closed for hours.

"So, both coffins empty, that makes three girls signed up for the army of zombies," Xander remarked.

"Is it an army if you only have three?" Willow wondered.

Buffy opened her mouth to respond, but before she could say anything, a deep voice, calm, with only a trace of bitterness spoke from the doorway. "You're back."

Angel was in the library, waiting. Buffy stared at him, her eyes registering so many emotions: the shame of being caught in a lie, the surprise of seeing him . . . and the shock of discovering Cordelia clinging to his arm, her head nearly buried in his strong chest.

"Angel . . . ," Buffy began as she walked toward him. She stopped just beside Xander—a fact that wasn't lost on Angel.

"Xander." Angel greeted the teen for Buffy's benefit only.

"Angel," Xander replied, equally unenthused.

Angel's eyes never left Buffy's. "I thought you were taking the night off," he alleged suspiciously.

"I was . . . going to," Buffy lied. "But at the last minute . . ."

Angel cut her off. "Cordelia told me the truth."

"As long as you're here, perhaps you can be of some help," Giles interrupted, trying to get back to business.

Buffy was grateful for the save. "We were investigating," she admitted. "Somebody's been stealing the bodies of dead girls."

"I know," Angel assured her. "We found some of them."

"Like two of the three?" Buffy asked.

Angel shook his head. "I mean like *some* of them, like parts."

"It was horrible," Cordelia told the others. She looked up at Angel gratefully. "Angel saved me from an arm. God, there were parts of everywhere. Why do

Cordelia Chase

"Somebody's after me! This is all about me! Me! Me! Me!"
—Cordelia

"I think anyone who cuts dead girls into pieces does not get the benefit of the doubt. Let's end this thing."—Buffy

Cordelia Chase

~

Alexander Harris

Daniel Osbourne

~

Willow Rosenberg

Lyle and Candy Gorch

"It's a clothes fluke, and that's what it is
and there'll BE no more fluking."—Xander

"Got hunted."—Cordelia

"[Xander] just . . . grows on
you, like a Chia Pet."—Cordelia

"—whatever, point is, I haven't even worked up a sweat. See in the end Buffy's good, but she's just the runner-up. I'M THE QUEEN. If I get mad, what do you think I'm gonna do to you?"—Cordelia

these terrible things always happen to me?"

"Karma." Xander coughed the word into his fist.

Willow looked toward the others. "Well, so much for the zombie theory."

"So much for all our theories," Giles corrected.

"I don't get it," Buffy commented. "Why dig up three bodies just to chop them up and throw them away again? It doesn't make sense. Especially from a time management standpoint."

"What I saw didn't add up to three whole girls," Angel told her, all business. "I think they kept some parts."

Buffy grimaced. "Could this get yuckier?"

"They probably kept them to eat," Willow suggested.

There ya go. "Question answered," Buffy replied.

"But why dispose of the remains here at the school?" Giles wondered.

Buffy considered that for a moment. "Maybe whoever did it had other business in the neighborhood. Like classes."

"Oh," Giles muttered, considering the consequences of that theory. Was it possible that these body part collectors attended Sunnydale High? Why not? Anything was possible at a school located over the Hellmouth.

"This was no hatchet job," Angel told Buffy. "Whoever made those incisions really knew what they were doing."

"Yes, well, really, what student here would be that well-versed in physiology?" Giles wondered.

"I can think of maybe five or six guys in the science club. And me," Willow offered.

Xander grinned. "Well, so come clean and promise never to do it again, and we'll call it a night."

The group stared at Xander with surprise.

"He joked," Xander assured them.

Buffy turned to Willow. "Why don't you get their locker numbers? We'll check them out."

"No," Cordelia moaned pitifully. "I want to go home now. I have to bathe and burn my clothes."

"You have to go?" Xander asked with relief and a decided lack of pity. "Ah. Keep in touch. Bye-bye."

"I don't want to go alone. I'm still fragile," Cordelia continued, looking up at Angel. "Can you take me?"

"I . . ." Angel glimpsed at Buffy, his eyes searching her face, waiting for her to object.

Buffy looked from Cordelia to Angel with surprise, but said nothing. Cordelia took that opportunity to clutch Angel's arm even tighter. "Great! I'll drive!" she exclaimed as she led him from the library.

"How about that?" Xander pondered as they left. "I always pegged him as a one-woman vampire."

Willow nudged Xander, trying to instill some sensitivity into her friend. But she needn't have bothered. Buffy was busy staring at the library door. She hadn't heard a thing since Angel left the room.

Willow led Xander and Buffy down the empty hallways of Sunnydale High. Giles hovered nervously behind them, watching as Willow stopped at the locker of one of her friends from the science club and used information from a computer printout to open the lock. "I hope you understand that as a school official, I can not condone this unauthorized search," he exclaimed officiously.

"Okay, your butt's covered," Buffy assured him. "You want to grab a locker?"

"Yes, of course," Giles said, as he moved to open the next locker on Willow's list.

Buffy stood beside the next locker on her list and smirked. "Okay, Eric, let's see what's on your naughty little mind," she murmured as she turned the combination lock.

As Buffy opened Eric's locker, Willow peered into another one nearby. Inside that locker was nothing besides some textbooks and a stack of science and nature magazines. "*Scientific American*," Will said as she pulled out one of the mags. Her eyes lit up. "Ooh. I haven't read this one!"

Giles peered into another locker. More textbooks, notebooks, and magazines. "Nothing remarkable here," he muttered.

Xander, however, was having a much more fruitful search through a locker across the hall. "Guys," he called out.

Willow put back the magazine and shut the locker door. She and Giles hurried to Xander's side. "Your friend, Chris Epps's locker," he told Willow as he opened the door wider so they could see inside.

Willow studied the stack of books inside the locker. "*Gray's Anatomy, Mortician's Desk Reference, Robicheaux's Guide to Muscles and Tendons*."

Giles reached into the locker and pulled out a

folded piece of newspaper. As he read the headline, he knew they'd found at least part of the puzzle. "'Tragic Accident Kills Three.'" It was an article about Meredith Todd and her friends. "Fair to say, Chris is involved," Giles commented.

"He's into corpses all right," Xander agreed. "But we still don't know why."

"Yes, we do," Buffy called from her spot beside Eric's locker. She opened the locker door wider and showed the others her hideous discovery. A picture of a girl was taped to the inside of the door. But this was no ordinary sexy pinup. This was a collage of various body parts and facial features cut from various magazines. Separately, the picture's eyes, nose, mouth, and other body parts were absolutely perfect. But when they were pasted together, the creature they formed was absolutely grotesque.

"*I guess, you'd say, what could make me feel this way? My girl . . .*" Eric sang out the Motown song gleefully. He was alway at his happiest when he was in the lab he and Chris had built together.

They'd taken over Sunnydale High's old science lab. It was the perfect place—old, abandoned, *forgotten*. And conveniently big enough to store everything they'd need to pull off the greatest science experiment in Sunnydale history.

The boys were creating their own perfect woman—out of dead body parts. In fact, right now, in the center of the dark, dank room was an old operating table. Their unfinished masterpiece—the partially constructed body of a teenage girl—lay under a sheet on the table.

Eric smiled broadly as he looked over at his buddy Chris. "How's my baby?"

Chris scowled as he checked his neatly arranged equipment. "She's not your baby."

Eric looked over at the operating table in the center of the room. "She's not gonna be anyone's baby if we don't finish it soon."

"I'm working on it," Chris insisted as he checked the stitches on the girl's thigh.

Eric began to hang his newly-developed photos on a line to dry. He smiled sadistically as he stared at the faces of the teenage girls before him, including Willow, Buffy, and Cordelia. "So am I, friend," Eric assured Chris. "So am I."

The next morning, Willow and Xander sat on the steps of Sunnydale High, watching as a trio of totally geeky guys eyed one of Cordelia's Cordettes. They didn't have a shot at ever getting to first base with the gorgeous girl, but that didn't stop them from dreaming.

As Buffy arrived at the school she hurried to meet up with her friends. "Any sign of our suspects?" Xander asked her.

"Not yet," Buffy replied. She sat down and took a look at the gaggle of gawking guys in the hallway. "I don't get it. Why would anyone want to make a girl?"

"You mean when there's so many pre-made ones just lying around?" Xander shrugged. "The things we do for love."

Buffy glared at him. "Love has nothing to do with

this." She wanted to make that perfectly clear.

Xander nodded. "Maybe not, but I'll tell you this: People don't fall in love with what's right in front of them. People want the dream, what they can't have. The more unattainable, the more attractive."

Irony, thy name is Xander, Buffy thought. His comment was an oblique reference to the mini-crush he had on her. Never mind that Willow had been wanting him in a major way since grade school. Like a typical man, he was blind to it.

"And for Eric, the unattainable would include everyone . . . that's *alive,*" Willow continued.

Buffy nodded and began to head down the stairs to class. Willow and Xander followed close behind. "Eric's sick enough to do something like this," Buffy agreed, "but what's up with Chris? He seems like a human person."

"I don't know," Willow told her honestly. "The thing with his brother was really hard on him. He talked a lot about death. Maybe he just wants to get one up on it."

"But it's not . . . doable, is it?" Buffy wondered hesitantly. "I mean, making someone from scraps? Actually making them live?"

Willow sighed. "If it is, my science project's definitely coming in second this year."

From the corner of his eye, Xander caught a glimpse of Giles standing alone by the door to the school building. He was obviously searching for someone special. "And speaking of love . . . ," Xander said, nudging the others.

"We were talking about the reanimation of dead tissue," Willow corrected him.

Xander scowled. "Do I deconstruct your segues? Yeesh."

Buffy marched over to the awkward librarian and smiled. "Hey, Giles."

"Oh. Yes. Hello," Giles replied, his eyes never leaving the sea of people.

"Still no sign of our mad doctors," Buffy reported.

"What?" Giles asked, distracted. "Oh. Corpses. Evil. Very good." Suddenly Giles's face broke into a small nervous smile. Buffy followed his eyes until she saw what he saw. There was Ms. Calendar, coming down the hall with a student.

Buffy smiled encouragingly. "Okay Giles, just remember. 'I'm feeling a thing, you're feeling a thing.' But personalize it."

"Personalize it?" Giles repeated nervously.

"She's a techno pagan, right?" Buffy reminded Giles of Ms. Calendar's fascination with both magick and computers. "Ask her to bless your laptop or something."

Giles looked at her with a sense of panic in his eyes.

Buffy grinned as she walked off. "Have fun."

Xander and Willow followed behind, each giving their librarian a pat on the back for luck.

"No. Don't leave me," Giles called after them. But it was no use. In a matter of seconds, the trio was gone, and Giles was face-to-face with Ms. Calendar.

"Good morning, Rupert."

Giles nodded nervously. "Ms. Calendar."

"Please, call me Jenny," she urged. "Ms. Calendar is my father."

But Jenny's humor was lost on Giles. "Jenny then." He cleared his throat as the two walked side-by-side through the halls of the school. "You know, Jenny, I don't mean to appear indecorous . . ." Giles rolled his eyes at his own ineptness. "No, not indecorous."

Jenny's eyes sparkled as she smiled. "Yes?" she asked him.

"Oh, dear . . . I . . . uh . . . that is." Giles frowned. The words just wouldn't leave his lips.

Jenny waited expectantly for Giles to continue. When he didn't, she smiled kindly. "Rupert, look, I have to get inside to set up the computer lab."

Giles nodded. It was do or die time. "Well, what I'm proposing is—" But Giles's invitation was halted by the ringing of the school bell. Suddenly kids appeared as if out of nowhere, all of them hurrying to their first class.

"Sorry," Jenny said as she walked into the computer lab. "I really have to go."

Giles nodded and sighed in defeat as she walked into the computer lab. "Idiot," he admonished himself angrily as he turned to leave.

Just then Giles heard Jenny's clear, lilting voice in the hallway. "Listen, if it's important, why don't you just tell me at the game?" she asked, poking her head from the computer lab doorway.

Giles stared at her with surprise. "You're going to the football game?"

"You seem surprised."

Giles blushed. "I guess I just assumed you spent your evening downloading incantations . . . casting bones."

"On game night? Are you nuts?" She paused for a moment, clearly enjoying Giles sudden discomfort. "I assume you're going too?"

Well, he hadn't planned on it. But if Jenny was going to be there . . . "Oh, uh, of course."

Jenny grinned. "So why don't we just go together?" She asked him. "I could pick you up after school, we could get something to eat on the way if you like. How do you feel about Mexican?"

Giles could manage nothing more than a weak twitchy nod. But that seemed to be enough.

"And whatever it is you want to tell me, you can tell me then, okay?" Jenny assured him.

"Okay . . . tonight then." As Jenny walked back into her classroom, Giles remained alone in the hall, clearly too in shock even to move. Then slowly a smile of self-satisfaction emerged on his face. "That went well, I think," he congratulated himself. As he turned and headed down the long hallway, there was just a small triumphant bounce in his step.

Willow sat in the school science room poring over anatomy books, trying to figure out just how Chris and Eric could possibly create a human life from—for lack of a better term—spare parts. "I still don't get how Chris could do it," Willow wondered. "Arresting cell deterioration is one thing, but . . ."

Xander frowned. When Willow started talking all sciencelike, he could feel his mind wandering off. He reached over and began to play with a plastic model of a human skull. He used his hands to move the jaw up and down. "Hello . . . I want to get a*head*."

But Willow wasn't biting. "Maybe an electrical current combined with an adrenaline boost," she continued, as she turned the pages in the science book.

Xander moved the plastic skull closer to Willow. "For the love of God, somebody scratch my nose!" he joked.

Before Xander could go any further with his talking head comedy routine, Buffy whisked her way into the science room. Xander could tell by the look on her face that she was in no mood for goofing around. She was all business.

"Well, it's official," Buffy announced. "Chris and Eric didn't come to school today."

"That's not a coincidence," Xander suggested.

Willow gulped. "Maybe they finished their project."

The trio was quiet a moment, each of them considering what that could mean.

"God, what if it worked?" Buffy asked finally. "What if that poor girl is walking around?"

"Uh, poor *girls,* technically," Xander interrupted.

"What could she be thinking?" Buffy continued.

"And what are they going to do with her?" Willow wondered.

"I don't think we have to worry about that just yet." The trio looked up as soon as they heard Giles's voice providing them with this new piece of information. Their eyes were all focused on his, waiting for him to explain.

"I contacted the police this morning about the remains," Giles explained. "They've just finished sorting through them. Apparently they found three heads in the dumpster."

"And they only had three girls," Buffy recalled.

"So they don't have the whole, uh, package," Willow deduced.

"Sounds like the heads must be no good," Xander suggested. He thought about that, recalling the girls' picture in the newspaper article they'd discovered in Chris's locker. "Hmmm. They seemed attractive enough to me."

Buffy, Giles, and Willow stared at Xander.

"Obviously, I'm not as sick as Chris and Eric," Xander finished quickly.

Giles turned his attention back to the case at hand. "Based on what the police put together, they're one step away from completing their masterpiece."

Willow glanced down at the plastic head Xander had been playing with. "One step," she murmured fearfully.

Chris and Eric, too, were very aware that they were only a single step from doing something no other human had ever done before: create a new human life from used parts. But time was running out. They stood in Chris's basement, arguing fervently.

"If we wait too long, the onset of atrophy in the limbs will be irreversible," Eric warned his friend.

"We can turn up the current. That'll buy us a day at least."

Eric shook his head. He knew Chris was simply stalling, trying desperately to put off the inevitable.

"We'll lose the entire body if we don't attach the head soon!"

"We have time!" Chris insisted.

But Eric wasn't buying it. They'd worked too hard, come too far. "We don't!" he told him. "The crash with the girls was lucky. But we can't keep waiting for another lucky accident to just drop a head in our laps. You know what we have to do." Eric folded his spindly arms across his chest and rolled his eyes. "Hell, it's just one lousy girl!"

Chris's eyes filled with tears as he considered what Eric was asking him to do. "I won't do it. . . . I can't. . . . I can't . . . kill anyone. Please understand. I can't do that. Please don't make me."

A figure emerged from behind a stack of old boxes. "But you gave me your word. . . . You promised me, *little brother*, that I wouldn't be alone."

Chris looked up helplessly at his very much alive older brother Daryl. Daryl was a hideously frightening soul. His skin had a distinctly gray pallor—he hadn't seen the light of day in more than a year. His many facial scars, each stitched by his younger brother's loving hand, were huge and rambling—like a patchwork quilt containing his eyes, nose, and mouth. The ragged, zig-zagging stitches had never really healed properly, so they appeared red and puffy against the backdrop of Daryl's gray-white skin.

Obviously Daryl couldn't very well go out of the house.

But Chris understood that living alone in the dark, dusty, crowded basement was slowly driving his older brother mad.

And Daryl wasn't the only one who had changed since his horrific accident. Eric, too, had developed a frightening side to his personality. It was almost as though he'd used Daryl's troubles to justify his own need for revenge against the beautiful girls who scorned him day in and day out.

"The body is perfect," Eric told Daryl, "and if we harvest a head tonight, she'll be ready by sunrise."

As Eric spoke, Daryl paced around the living room like a caged animal, stopping right in front of his younger brother. The tall, muscular former football star crouched down so he could look his brother in the eye. "When you brought me back, you promised you'd take care of me," Daryl reminded Chris. "I need this, Chris. I need someone."

"Please don't ask me to do this," Chris begged. "Don't ask me to take a life."

"I tried to tell him, if you take a life to make a new life, the whole thing's a wash," Eric assured Daryl. "No harm no foul."

Chris looked pleadingly into his brother's eyes. "Maybe you could . . . you could go out," Chris suggested gently. "Let people know."

A look of both fear and furor came over Daryl's scarred face. "No! Can't see me!" he shouted angrily. But in a moment the outrage was gone from his tone. He looked pleadingly at his brother. "Chris, you've always been smarter than me. You were always the brains. You're the only one who can help me."

Chris stared at his older brother uncertainly. Despite his claims, Daryl was quite smart himself—

smart enough to see his brother's hesitation. He began an old chant, one he heard all the time when he was a football hero—when he was whole. "Third and long, seconds to go! Where do you throw, where do you throw?"

"Number five," Chris continued the cheer quietly. "Daryl's gonna drive."

"Help me, Brother," Daryl begged.

Chris nodded ever so slightly.

A look of relief rose in Daryl's eyes. He clutched his younger brother and kissed the top of his head. Then he turned his attentions toward Eric. "Show me!"

Eric smiled triumphantly and removed three black-and-white photos from his backpack. He watched with glee as Daryl carefully surveyed the photos, choosing the girl who would share his exile. Finally he pointed to one of the photos. "This one."

Eric smiled at the photo. "A man of taste," he complimented Daryl. Then he grabbed a pair of scissors and began to snip away at the photo. "*Talkin 'bout my girl,*'" he sang fiendishly, as he carefully cut Cordelia's head from her body.

Buffy paced up and down the library floor. The stress was clearly getting to her. She knew that Chris and Eric were going to strike, and soon. The question was, could she stop them before they completed their ghoulish science project?

"Well, I've checked the obits," Willow told her as she scanned the computer screen. "Nothing that would make for a likely candidate."

"They're kinda picky for guys who had three heads to begin with," Xander noted.

"Formaldehyde," Willow muttered.

Xander stared at her. *Talk about a weird non sequitur.* "Come again?"

"Yes, of course," Giles agreed. "It accelerates neural decay in the brain cells."

"A couple of days and they're useless," Willow told him. "They're gonna need something really fresh."

"How fresh?" Buffy asked, her voice becoming quietly alarmed.

"As fresh as possible," Willow began matter-of-factly. Then, suddenly she caught Buffy's drift. She looked up at her friend with a new sense of panic. "Buffy, you don't think they'd . . ."

"I think anyone who cuts dead girls into pieces does not get the benefit of the doubt," Buffy informed her. "Let's end this thing, now."

"Seconded," Giles agreed.

Immediately Buffy took charge of the situation. She turned to Willow and Xander. "You two head to Eric's. I'll try Chris's."

Giles looked sheepishly at Buffy. "I'm supposed to be at the, uh, the 'big game,' I believe it's called," he stammered.

Buffy fought off a grin. "You go ahead. We can handle this."

But Giles wasn't sure. "Well, this is my . . . I really should . . ."

"It's okay," Buffy assured him. "We'll meet up there. Report back."

"All right," Giles agreed.

As Buffy headed for the door, Willow hurried to catch up with her. "Buffy, don't be too hard on Chris," she asked her friend. "I mean, he's not a vampire."

But Buffy could find no pity for Chris in her heart. "No. He's just a ghoul."

• • •

Buffy was surprised when Chris's mother opened the door to the Eppses' home. The woman looked as though she hadn't bathed or brushed her hair in months. Her plaid flannel shirt was faded and wrinkled, much like her sad face. In the background, Buffy could hear a video of a high school football game playing on the TV.

"I'm a friend of Chris's," Buffy told Mrs. Epps. "I need to talk to him. Do you know if he's home?"

Without a word, Chris's mother turned and walked inside the house. Buffy followed her into a musty living room and watched as the woman settled into a well-worn easy chair and flicked her cigarette into an over-flowing ashtray. Mrs. Epps stared at the TV, seeming not to notice that Buffy was even there.

Buffy looked around the room. It had been turned into a shrine of sorts. The walls were papered with pho-tos of Daryl Epps in his football uniform, running across the field and leaping up to catch passes. Football trophies lined the mantle, and newspaper articles chron-icling Daryl's on-field successes were framed and placed around the room. Buffy was struck by just how gorgeous Daryl had been. No wonder Cordelia had had a thing for him.

"So . . . is Chris home?" Buffy asked Mrs. Epps again.

But Chris's mom didn't answer. Instead, she pointed toward the TV screen. "Westbury game. November 17, '95," she explained to Buffy. "Daryl was rushed 185 yards that night. Four TDs. He was MVP and made All-City that season."

Buffy glanced at the video and watched as Daryl ran across the field. A stack of videotapes sat atop the TV, each one labeled with the date and names of football teams.

"Yeah, that was a great one," Buffy agreed, trying not to upset Mrs. Epps. "But is Chris home?"

Mrs. Epps's eyes never left the screen. "I don't know," she said. "Is this a school day?" Before Buffy could reply, the woman leaned closer to the TV screen. "Watch this move," she told Buffy. "Daryl takes the kick off, sheds one-two-three defenders! He breaks into the open field for a ninety-five yard touchdown."

Quietly Buffy backed out of the room. As she made her way toward the bedrooms, Buffy could hear Mrs. Epps's tragic voice. "He would have been nineteen next week, you know," she said in a strangely matter-of-fact voice.

The first door Buffy came to was papered in signs. Some read NO TRESPASSING, others KEEP OUT and NO ADMITTANCE. As far as Buffy was concerned, that was an open invitation to enter the room.

As she headed down the stairs toward the basement, Buffy's body instinctively got into ready mode. Her heart beat just a little faster, and her muscles flexed, ready for anything they might come up against.

But there was no one in the basement. At least no one Buffy could see. Just some old boxes and furniture.

Quickly her eyes darted around the room, expertly searching for some clue that someone—or something—had been there.

As she looked over at a chest of drawers, she noticed a pile of photos on top. She went over and glanced at them. She flipped through them quickly, only shivering slightly when she saw her own image in the pile. Then she came to the photo Eric had cut up not long before. Buffy couldn't tell who she was—her head and hair were missing.

Then she noticed a drawing of a woman's body on the table. Every muscle, tendon, vein, and artery was expertly rendered, as though it had come straight from a textbook. And pasted to the top of the drawing was a teenage girl's head.

"Cordelia," Buffy whispered quietly to herself.

A large, scarred teenager emerged from behind a pile of boxes. Despite his size, Daryl was able to move so quietly that Buffy didn't seem to notice his presence. Instead she noticed the loud creaking noise coming from the floorboards above. Someone was coming. Quickly Buffy leaped up, grabbed onto an overhead water pipe, and swung herself out of an open window.

Daryl's lonely, angry eyes followed her as she left his lair.

Cordelia, of course, was totally oblivious to the gruesome fate that awaited her. She was busy giving her makeup a last minute touch-up before she ran out onto the field, ready to cheer the Sunnydale team to victory.

"Cordelia, you coming?" One of the other cheer-leaders called as she left the locker room.

"I'll be right out," Cordelia assured her while she expertly applied another stroke of lip gloss. As she looked into the mirror to admire herself, Cordelia saw a male figure in the reflection. She jumped, and then took a breath as she realized who it was.

"Oh, Chris," she said with relief. "Hi. God, you scared me."

Chris just stared at her. The conflicting emotions were bubbling inside so badly that he could barely breathe.

"What are you doing here?" Cordelia asked him.

Chris winced painfully.

"Is something wrong?"

Chris didn't answer her. Instead he stepped aside, giving Eric room to step in and slam a cloth sack down over Cordelia's head. Cordelia screamed, but there was no one left in the locker room to hear her.

Buffy raced up the stairs toward the girls' locker room. She had to warn Cordelia about Eric and Chris's awful plan. As she was climbing up, two cheerleaders were on their way down toward the field. Buffy stopped them in their tracks. "Joy, Lisa, where's Cordelia?"

Joy shook her head. "Cordelia's got a game to think about. She doesn't need losers like you—"

Buffy didn't have time to debate. The Slayer pow-erfully slapped her hands against the wall, one on either side of the perky cheerleader, effectively fencing her in. Joy opened her eyes wide with surprise.

"I'm sorry," Buffy said, her voice dripping with false sweetness. "Where did you say?"

That was all it took to get the information she needed. Quickly Buffy raced off toward the locker room, leaving Joy and Lisa to deal with their surprise at her forcefulness.

As Buffy entered the room she discovered Cordelia struggling wildly on the floor as Eric attempted to tie her hands behind her back. Instantly Buffy went into Slayer mode, leaping up in the air and heel kicking Eric away from his prisoner.

Eric was not prepared for a fight. Instead he beat a quick retreat, dashing out a back door.

Buffy reached down and removed the cloth sack from Cordelia's face. "It's okay, you're okay," Buffy assured her. "He's gone."

"Oh, my God! Buffy!" Cordelia cried out.

"He's gone," Buffy assured her again, as she helped pull the cheerleader to her feet. "What happened?"

Cordelia struggled to catch her breath. "I don't know," she gasped. "I was just about to go to the field when Chris came in, and then somebody just jumped me."

Buffy's eyes scanned the locker room, but it seemed empty. "Well, it's okay now," she repeated. "You're fine. Just take your time."

Cordelia was silent for a moment, listening. The marching band was beginning to play.

"Oh, my God! That's the fight song." Cordelia exclaimed. "It's time for the cheerleader pyramid at mid-field. I have to go."

"Are you sure you're okay to go out there?" Buffy asked incredulously.

"You don't understand. I have to go. I'm the apex." And with that, Cordelia grabbed her pom-poms and raced out onto the field, leaving Buffy to marvel—once again—at Cordelia's unique sense of priorities.

Now Buffy was alone in the locker room. The quiet was eerie, almost deafening. And still, Buffy could sense that someone else was there, listening . . . waiting.

"I know what you're trying to do, Chris," Buffy called out finally. "You and Eric." She waited a second, but no one answered. Still, Buffy was certain Chris hadn't left. "I know about the bodies from the cemetery," she continued. "But you haven't hurt anyone yet."

Slowly, quietly, Chris stepped out from behind a row of lockers. Buffy was amazed at just how small and vulnerable he seemed. His eyes looked tired and tortured.

"Listen, I don't know what it's like to lose someone close to you," Buffy admitted quietly. "But what you're trying to do is wrong."

"I have to do it for him. He needs someone." Chris seemed to be justifying everything to himself as well as to Buffy.

"Who? Eric?" Buffy asked. "He needs industrial strength therapy."

"He always looked out for me . . . stood up for me. . . . He's all alone. . . . Everybody loved him, and now he's all alone. . . ."

Buffy listened to Chris for a moment, trying to make sense of what he was saying. Then, as it all became clear, her green eyes opened wide with a sense of fear and astonishment. "Oh, my God."

As his old team ran out onto the field in search of victory, Daryl was in his lair, spinning out of control. The adrenaline that surged through his angry veins had made him stronger than ever before. The former football star yanked bookshelves from the wall and heaved them across the room, slamming them to the ground with such power that the metal shelving cracked in half. Eric stood across the room, watching him with fear . . . and fascination.

"He promised me! Promised!" Daryl screamed as he threw a large metal rack across the room. "I wouldn't have to be alone."

"It's not too late," Eric said suddenly.

The sound of Eric's voice reminded Daryl that he was not alone in the basement. Instantly the former football player turned and grabbed Eric by the collar. Eric was small and scrawny; it took no effort at all for Daryl to lift his spindly little body off the ground. Eric gulped as he stared into Daryl's eyes—one blue, the other green.

"Nothing's changed," Eric assured Daryl, his voice quaking slightly as he struggled to hold onto his life. "We can still do this. You and me."

Daryl breathed heavier, but he did not loosen his grip on Eric's shirt. There was no telling what was going through his mind. Eric knew he had to explain himself, and quickly. "Your brother's not the only one who can create life," Eric boasted. "What do you say?"

As the meaning of Eric's words became clearer to Daryl, the former running back loosened his grip on the boy's collar. He slowly lowered Eric to the ground.

As he looked up at Daryl, a creepy smile of enthusiasm grew across Eric's lips. This was just what he'd been hoping for.

"Let's go scare you up a date."

• • •

By the time Buffy and Chris arrived in Daryl's basement lair, he and Eric were long gone. The only sign that they'd been there were the piles of damaged books and broken shelves Daryl had left behind in his fit of anger.

"Okay, he's not here. Where else could he be?" Buffy demanded of Chris.

Chris shook his head. "But he would never go out," he assured Buffy. Then the expression on his face changed to one of fear. "Unless . . ."

"He's gonna pick up where you left off," Buffy finished his thought.

Giles smiled uncomfortably as he and Jenny Calendar stumbled through the school's bleachers at the start of the football game. He seemed out of place in his tweed jacket and tie, uncomfortably carrying pennants, soda, and popcorn through the throngs of screaming students and parents.

"I don't know what it is about football that does it for me," Jenny mused out loud as she sat down in one of the seats. "I mean it lacks the grace of basketball, the poetry of baseball. At its best, it's unadorned aggression. It's just such a rugged contest."

Giles chuckled. "Rugged? American football?"

Jenny looked at him curiously. "And that's funny because?"

Giles shrugged. "I do find it odd that a nation that prides itself on its virility feels compelled to strap on forty pounds of protective gear just to play rugby."

"Is this your normal strategy for a first date? Dissing my country's national pastime?"

Giles was surprised at her statement. "Did you say . . . 'date'?" he asked her with a sense of bewilderment.

Jenny leaned back triumphantly. "You noticed that, huh?" she remarked with a grin.

Suddenly Giles felt as inexperienced as a British schoolboy. But he barely had a moment to enjoy the emotion before Willow and Xander appeared before him.

"Hi, Ms. Calendar," Willow greeted the computer teacher. "Hey, Giles."

"Hi, guys," Ms. Calendar replied. "What's up?"

"Eric's was a bust," Willow replied, reporting on their scouting expedition in Eric's room. "Nothing there."

"Yeah, nothing but a lot of computer equipment and a pornography collection so prodigious it even scared me," Xander noted.

"Buffy get back yet?" Willow asked Giles.

"No," he told her. Then he added hopefully, "Perhaps you should circulate down nearer the field to find her."

But if Willow and Xander got the hint, they weren't playing. Instantly the two took seats right in front of Giles and Ms. Calendar and settled in to watch the game.

"So . . . what's the score?" Xander asked as he grabbed the popcorn container from Giles's hands and scarfed down a handful.

But Giles was right. Xander and Willow should have been closer to the field. That was where Eric and Daryl were lying in wait, ready to capture Cordelia as soon as she left the field.

Daryl stood under the stands watching as the Sunnydale Razorbacks took the ball and ran toward the goal line. His lower lip quivered slightly as he viewed the game from beneath the stands. That should have been him on the field, running for the touchdown for some college team that was honored to have him. But Daryl had to hide instead. He was too hideous to be seen. And he was tired of being so alone.

As Daryl caught sight of Cordelia leaving the field in search of water, he moved quickly beneath the bleachers toward the side of the field. No sooner had Cordelia drawn herself a cup of water than Daryl grabbed her from behind and jerked her into the darkness below the bleachers.

Cordelia screamed wildly, but no one heard her. The Razorbacks had just scored; the crowd's cheers drowned her out.

Instantly the other cheerleaders went into a new routine, not seeming to notice that Cordelia was gone. But Buffy noticed. She and Chris had arrived at the game and were scanning the field for Cordelia.

"I don't see her. Do you?" Buffy asked Chris hopefully.

But Chris didn't see Cordelia anywhere. And they both knew that could mean only one thing.

Cordelia lay on the white gurney in the old science lab, struggling wildly as Eric bound her hands to the sides of the bed. "Please. . . . What's going on?" she begged. "Take off the blindfold. I won't scream. I promise."

But Eric didn't remove the black scarf from her eyes. Instead he let her lie there in the darkness, while he prepared things on the other side of the lab.

Daryl went over toward a second gurney and lifted the white sheet that covered the headless body Chris and Eric had created. "She's beautiful," he murmured.

Eric hurried over, took the sheet from Daryl's hands, and swiftly covered the torso. "No. It's bad luck for the groom to see the bride before the wedding," he reminded Daryl.

All this strange talk was making Cordelia more afraid than ever. Where was she? Who were these maniacs? *And what bride?* "Please, just take off the blindfold. I promise I won't scream," Cordelia begged her captors once again.

Daryl turned toward the frightened cheerleader. "Cordelia," he said quietly as he removed the black scarf from her eyes.

Cordelia took one look at Daryl's hideously scarred face and let out a blood curdling cry.

Eric laughed. "You can scream all you want," he told her. "We're in an abandoned building."

Cordelia didn't disappoint. She screamed again. Her cries were louder and more painful this time. Eric picked up a heavy metal tray and waved it menacingly above her head. "Okay. That's enough," he ordered threateningly. Instantly Cordelia stopped yelling.

Daryl looked down at Cordelia. A sudden tenderness came over his mangled, stitched face. "You were always good to me. Always noticed me, but I ignored you," Daryl told her as he gently stroked her silky, brown hair with his rough, patched hand. "I'm sorry. I'm glad that I got this second chance to tell you that."

Cordelia studied the tall, monster-like teen that stood before her. "D-Daryl?" she asked him, stunned.

"I was thoughtless," Daryl continued. "I know that now. But I've changed. I've learned to appreciate how much it meant that you wanted to be with me."

Eric walked over towards Cordelia's head. "We're ready," he told Daryl playfully.

"Ready? Ready for what?" Cordelia demanded.

Eric smiled. "You're going to feel a little pinch, maybe a little discomfort around the neck area," he said, sounding every bit like a mad doctor. "But when you wake up, you'll have the body of a seventeen-year-old."

Eric crossed over and lifted the sheet from the body he and Chris had created, making sure Cordelia had a clear view of the arms and limbs that would soon be hers.

"In fact, you'll have the body of several."

Cordelia screamed even louder.

Buffy stood beside the bleachers just a few feet from where Cordelia had been kidnapped only minutes ago. Her trained eyes scanned the area, looking for some sort of clue as to where Cordelia could be. Then she saw two yellow and blue pom-poms lying on the dirt beside the water cooler. She bent down and picked one up. "He was here," she told Chris. "Where did he take her?"

"To the rest of the body. To the lab." Chris couldn't look Buffy in the eye. She looked so fierce, so determined. He couldn't help wondering what she would do to his brother if she found him.

"Where is that?" Buffy demanded.

Chris didn't want to answer. "I promised him," he tried to explain.

Buffy flung the pom-poms on the ground. She was losing patience. "He'll kill Cordelia." She eyed Chris desperately. "You can't just give and take lives like that. It's not your job."

For a moment, Chris didn't say anything. He wanted to help his brother. And yet . . . "He's in the old science building. Everything is set up there," he admitted finally.

"Find Willow and Xander and Mr. Giles. Tell them what's going on," Buffy commanded as she raced off to stop Daryl from turning Cordelia into a modern-day bride of Frankenstein. Chris waited only a second before he went in search of Buffy's friends. Deep down he knew he had no choice, no matter what he'd promised Daryl. Things had already gone too far.

Eric smiled as he emptied the contents of a five-gallon drum of gasoline into the lab generator. Within seconds the hum of machinery filled the room. It was time to finish what they'd started.

"Daryl, please," Cordelia begged. "You don't have to do this."

"I have to," Daryl told her, "so we can be together."

Cordelia was growing frantic now. Eric was already running a sharp blade through a Bunsen burner flame, sterilizing it for the operation. "We can be together anyway," she assured Daryl. "I'll be with you. I promise."

Daryl leaned over so Cordelia could get a good look at the patchwork quilt that was his face. "See anything you like?" he asked in a voice so cruel and cold it made her shiver.

When Cordelia didn't—*couldn't*—answer, Daryl turned toward the body of the unfinished girl on the next gurney. He lifted the sheet and showed Cordelia her new body. "When you're finished, you won't go out. You won't run away," Daryl predicted. "We'll hide together."

Tears began to flow down Cordelia's face. "Please . . . ," she begged.

But Eric wasn't one to show mercy. He walked over toward the gurney and showed the cheerleader the newly sterilized metal blade. "Sterile enough for government work," he assured Cordelia as he lowered the blade to her neck.

And then, suddenly, there was a loud crashing noise as Buffy kicked open the door and moved purposefully across the lab.

"Buffy! Help me!" Cordelia cried out.

As Buffy stared down at Cordelia, Eric took his knife and threw it straight for Buffy's heart. But the Slayer was quick. In a single, swift motion she caught the knife by its handle in midair. Eric, ever the coward, fled into the corner and ducked down.

Buffy focused on Daryl, trying to appeal to whatever humanity was left inside him. "Daryl, listen, I know what you're doing," Buffy explained. "Your brother sent me to stop you."

Daryl stared at her in complete disbelief. "No. He wouldn't do that."

"Buffy, they're crazy!" Cordelia shouted from the gurney.

"It's okay, Cordelia," Buffy assured her, without ever taking her eyes from Daryl's. "I'm getting you out of here."

"No! I'm not done with her yet!" Daryl shouted. He picked up a sharp surgical saw from the tray and reached down toward Cordelia's neck. "I'M NOT FINISHED!"

Buffy leaped toward Daryl and kicked him away from Cordelia. But years of football had left Daryl strong and quick. He'd suffered far worse than a kick like that. He stood his ground and punched Buffy hard, sending her reeling into the Cordelia's gurney. The Slayer rolled over Cordelia and quickly regained her footing. She pulled back her arm, ready to punch. But Daryl was fast. He pounced on Buffy. Cordelia's gurney rolled backward across the room, knocking over the can of gasoline. Instantly whatever gas was left in the jug spilled out onto the floor.

"Buffy!" Cordelia cried out helplessly.

"I won't live alone!" Daryl declared as he made a move towards Buffy.

Just then Eric made a break for the door. "I'm getting out of here," he told himself as he ran.

But there was no way Daryl was letting that happen. They'd come too far to stop now. Daryl needed Eric to fulfill Chris's promise. The former football star grabbed the scrawny science nerd by the scruff of the neck and lifted him in the air. "You have to help me," he demanded.

"Let go," Eric begged, as his legs dangled wildly over the floor.

Daryl was beyond reason. Furiously he hurled Eric across the room, slamming the boy's thin, meek body against a cement wall. Eric slid to the floor, unconscious.

Buffy made a quick lunge toward Cordelia. But before she could reach the gurney, Daryl dove at the Slayer. Instantly Buffy raised her leg and landed a swift roundhouse kick to his gut. The powerful move sent Daryl reeling. He plowed into a nearby table and knocked Eric's Bunsen burner to the ground.

The pain should have driven the beast to his knees, but Daryl was beyond pain now. He was all fury and power. He grabbed a bottle of chemicals and hurled it right at Buffy. Daryl was so intent on killing her, he never noticed the flame of the Bunsen burner behind him as it lit the spilled gasoline into a raging fire.

But Buffy saw the flames—they were moving dangerously close to Cordelia. If she didn't get to her soon . . .

Before Buffy could finish the thought, Xander burst through the doors of the lab. "Buffy!" he cried out.

"Get Cordelia," Buffy ordered, as she focused her energy on Daryl, kicking him with blow after blow from her sharp boots.

It was only a moment more before Chris, Giles, Jenny, and Willow appeared at the lab. The flames were higher now, lapping up everything in their path. It was clear that the others could do nothing to help Cordelia; it was all up to Xander now.

Xander looked around for a way out, but flames blocked his path in all directions—like some sort of sick maze with no real complete pathway. There was only one thing for him to do. Quickly he grabbed the gurney, gave it a massive shove toward the door, and leaped on top of Cordelia.

"Noooooo!" Cordelia cried out as the flames rose up around her and Xander. She was certain they were both about to be burned alive.

Miraculously Cordelia and Xander managed to roll their way to the door without a single burn. And Willow and Giles had managed to drag Eric to safety as well. Not that he deserved it or anything.

But it was clear to everyone involved that the Scooby Squad's work wasn't finished.

"Buffy, get out!" Jenny cried.

Before Buffy could make a dash toward the door, Daryl struck again, using a single motion to slam her to the floor. As she lay there, helpless, Daryl grabbed an old metal desk and waved it above her head. He was about to smash the metal into her head, when a voice cried out.

"Daryl! Don't!"

Daryl looked across the fiery lab at his younger brother. He knew what a sacrifice Chris had made for him. He had tried to save his life. But somehow Chris's heroic deed had turned him into a monster. And that was something Daryl could not bear being. A sudden last burst of humanity seem to come over him. He moved away, rather than kill Buffy. Then he stared at the flames that were about to engulf his headless bride. He couldn't stand the pain of seeing his last hope for a partner burn away.

"No! She's mine!" the scarred teen cried out painfully as he barreled through the flames and fell onto the body, trying desperately to shield it from a fiery end.

But there was no chance of saving her now. In an instant the fire completely consumed Daryl, as well as the lifeless body beneath him. Instinctively Chris tried to reach his brother, to save him one more time. Buffy leaped to her feet and grabbed him, pulling him to safety.

As Buffy and Chris left the inferno, Daryl's huge body became motionless. This time, not even Chris's scientific mind would be able to save him.

Buffy sat beside Chris on the hood of a police car, watching the Sunnydale Fire Department struggle to put out the blaze. Chris stared at the flames, unable to turn away from where he'd last seen his brother alive.

"The first time he woke up, after . . . he said I shouldn't have brought him back," Chris explained to Buffy. "I was just trying to look out for him. Like he would have done for me."

Buffy struggled for something to say, something kind and comforting. Instead she rested a supportive hand on his shoulder to let him know she understood.

As she looked out into the darkness, Buffy saw a

familiar, muscular figure emerge from the night. "I saw the fire," Angel said as he approached her. "Figured you'd be here. Is everyone okay?"

"Yeah, we're okay," she said gently, looking into Angel's eyes, hoping that they, too, were okay now.

Giles walked over to Jenny Calendar and handed her a cup of hot coffee. "I'm sorry about all this," he apologized.

"That's okay," Jenny assured him, taking a sip of the hot drink. "Although a good rule of thumb for a first date is don't do anything so exciting that it will be hard to top on the second date."

"Believe it or not, since I've moved here to live on top of the Hellmouth, the events of this evening actually qualify as a slow night," he explained ruefully. Then he stopped and looked at her curiously. "Did you say, 'second date'?"

Jenny laughed. "Ah. You noticed, huh?"

Xander watched as Buffy and Angel made eyes at each other, and Giles blushed like a fool with Jenny Calendar. "Well, I guess that makes it official. Everyone's paired off. Vampires can get dates. Hell even the school librarian is seeing more action than me," he complained to Willow. "You ever feel like the world is a giant game of musical chairs and the music stopped and we're the only ones who don't have a chair?"

"All the time," Willow assured him.

"Xander," Cordelia interrupted as she walked over toward him. Her face was covered in soot, and her cheerleading uniform would need a good cleaning, but other than that, she was unscathed. "I . . . uh . . . just wanted to thank you for saving my life in there. It was really brave and heroic and all. And if there's ever anything I can do to . . ." She stopped, hesitantly. *Gratitude, never really been my thing.*

"Do you mind?" Xander barked at her. "We're talking here."

Cordelia's face registered shock and surprise. She'd been making an honest, heartfelt thank you, and Xander had just totally blown her off. She turned and walked away.

Xander turned his attention back to Willow. "So, where were we?"

Willow looked from Xander to Cordelia, noting the irony in the whole situation. "Wondering why we never seem to have dates," she reminded Xander.

"Oh, yeah. So, why do you think that is?"

It was a little before dawn when the fire trucks finally pulled away from the old lab. Buffy and Angel left together and headed toward the quiet of the cemetery.

"The whole thing was creepy. But at the same time . . . I mean he did do it all for his brother," Buffy explained to Angel.

"Sounds like he took it a little over the edge."

Buffy considered that for a moment. "Love makes you do the wacky," she figured.

"The what?"

"Crazy stuff."

Angel sighed. "Oh. Crazy like a 241-year-old being jealous of a high school junior?"

Buffy smiled. *Gotta love the vulnerability.* "Are you fessing up?"

"I thought about it," Angel admitted. "Maybe he bothers me a little."

Buffy stopped walking and turned to face Angel. She needed to make him understand. "I don't love Xander," she assured him.

"But he's in your life. He gets to be there when I can't. Take your classes, eat your meals, hear your jokes and complaints." He stopped and looked woefully at the dark sky above. "He gets to see you in the sunlight."

"I don't look all that great in direct light."

That brought a slight smile to Angel's otherwise serious face. He looked up again at the sky. "It'll be morning soon."

Buffy knew what that meant. "I should probably go," she said quietly, looking up at him with painful eyes. She didn't want this moment to end. And yet, she knew it had to.

"I could walk you home."

Angel reached out and gently took Buffy's small hand in his own. Slowly they strolled through the cemetery, so engrossed in each other they didn't even realize they'd just passed the grave of Daryl Epps.

1978–1996.

REST IN PEACE.

"Homecoming"

Cordelia leaned back into her chair at the Bronze and took a sip of her drink. To the average person just wandering in, it would seem as though nothing had changed since that time last year, when Cordelia had been hanging out at the club with Mitch Fargo. There was Cordelia, sitting right in the center of the action, impeccably dressed, settling into the arm of a studly guy.

But Cordelia knew a lot had changed since then. Her senior year at Sunnydale High had been totally unpredictable. For starters, the hottie who was currently nuzzling her long, slender neck wasn't the captain of the baseball team, the basketball team, or even the tennis team. No, Cordelia's new guy was Xander Harris.

No one had found it harder to believe that Cordelia could be attracted to Xander than Cordelia herself. But their intense fighting eventually turned to intense smooching, and now the two of them were an item. At first Cordelia had been petrified that her friends would find out about her relationship with him, but lately she'd decided that didn't matter. As Cordy had explained to her friends, "I'll date whoever the hell I want to date, no matter how lame he is."

Some of those friends had found that too hard to bear. But Cordelia didn't mind. Despite her misgivings, she was constantly finding herself more drawn to the Scooby Squad. Cordelia herself had slain a few vamps and found it gross, scary, and oddly compelling.

Cordelia wasn't the only new vampire warrior at Sunnydale High. Recently a new slayer, Faith, had arrived at the Hellmouth. Faith was sort of the anti-Buffy. She was wild, forceful, and seemed to have no loyalties or emotions whatsoever. Cordy wasn't sure how she felt about Faith. She was totally brave, sure, but could you trust someone so . . . goth?

Senior year hadn't only been a banner year for Cordelia. As she looked out onto the dance floor, Cordy could see Willow bopping joyfully to the sounds of the Bronze's hottest new band, Dingoes Ate My Baby. Willow's new stud-man, Oz, was the lead guitarist. Cordelia had to admit that Oz was kind of cute—in that punk-rock werewolf way. Cordy herself wasn't into guys who howled at the moon. But for someone like Willow, well . . . a guy who turned into a werewolf was better than no guy at all. Besides, Willow helped Oz restrain himself on nights of the full moon, so that worked out okay for them.

Cordelia looked over toward the coffee bar, where

she saw Buffy chatting with Scott Hope, an extremely smoochable member of their senior class. Buffy was pretending going through the motions with Scott, but Cordy could tell the Slayer was distracted—as usual. In fact Buffy had been distracted for months, ever since she'd had to slay Angel in order to seal the mouth of Acathla and stop the world from certain destruction. Scott was cute enough, certainly not Cordy-worthy, but fine for Buffy. And he did have one advantage over Angel: He was human!

It had been just before Halloween—*ironic much?*— when Buffy had first clued Cordy to the fact that Angel was a vampire, and not just an unbelievably gorgeous older stud. (Well, he was older, for sure, but Cordelia hadn't figured on more than 200 years older!) Still, the discovery that Angel was a vamp wasn't a total shock. After all, who else but a member of the undead would choose Buffy Summers over Cordelia?

Of course, Angel wasn't your typical vamp. He had once had a soul and a conscience, the result of a curse from a band of Gypsies who were out for revenge after Angel had killed one of their own. Giving him back his soul had been the ultimate revenge. Angel's curse was to have done hideous things, and to feel guilt for doing them. The pain of it nearly drove him mad.

But the Gypsy curse had a second facet of which Angel was not aware. If the vamp ever got too happy, he'd lose his soul and go back to his former, evil self.

Buffy made Angel happy. Perfectly happy. Which meant that she made him really evil. Once Angel found happiness, the curse was broken. After one night of passion with Buffy, Angel was no longer a cuddly vamp. He was just another savage creature from Hell. *That must've been one heck of a horizontal hustle!* Cordy frowned. It was always the quiet ones who turned into animals in bed . . . or in the case of Angel, after they got out of bed.

The newly vicious vamp then went on a killing spree. One of his victims was Giles's lady-love Jenny Calendar.

Before Angel could kill everyone else Buffy cared about—not to mention the Slayer herself—Willow came up with a way to give Angel his soul back. Unfortunately, by then Buffy had learned that she had to kill Angel in order to seal the portal.

Talk about an ugly breakup.

Cordy sighed. Senior year, so far, had had its challenges: zombies, a hideous cloven-hoofed, milky-eyed creature named Kakistos, and a particularly vicious— yet stylish—vamp named Mr. Trick, to name just a few. But for the most part it was a lot of fun. And now it was almost time for another homecoming queen competition. *Her very last.* Cordelia's thoughts turned to what color dress she'd wear and how wonderful the new tiara would feel on her head—after she'd been named Homecoming Queen. Cordelia was certain she'd win the contest. No matter how much things had changed at Sunnydale High, *some* things always remained the same.

Buffy sat at the coffee bar of the Bronze and played

with her biscotti. Around her, she could hear the cheerful banter of her friends, but her mind was far away. She was distracted and more than a little stressed.

But no one else seemed to notice. They were all too caught up in their homecoming plans. "I think we should get a limo," Cordelia suggested to the others. A pink flush rose in her cheeks, making her more gorgeous than usual. Cordy always got a happy glow when she thought about dances, gowns, and limos.

Xander, however, did not share her enthusiasm. "A limo?" he asked nervously. "A big, expensive limo?"

"That sounds like fun," Willow remarked. "And it is our last homecoming dance. Maybe we should make it a big deal."

Xander was getting more nervous now. Usually he could count on Will as an ally, but now she was obviously on the opposing team. "You want to talk fun?" he jabbered nervously. "Public bus. You meet the funnest people! Back me up here, Oz."

"Well, if it's a dollar issue, we could all take my van," Oz suggested, in an attempt to help his buddy out.

But Cordelia wasn't having it. "Van?" she asked, her voice slightly moving up the scales. "The Homecoming Queen does not go to the dance in a van. Use your head."

"Well, technically you haven't been elected yet . . . ," Xander began. He stopped mid thought, as Cordelia's deep hazel eyes shot angrily through him with laserlike accuracy. "Although you certainly and without a doubt will." He turned to the others. "Who else likes a limo?" It was hard for him to deny Cordy anything, particularly when she was wearing that sexy brown sleeveless shirt that made her neck look extra long.

Willow's eyes grew dreamy. "A private limo. . . . It is pretty cuddlesome." She turned toward Buffy. "If we all split the cost . . . ," she began.

"Maybe," Buffy said quietly, "if I go and all."

Willow's eyes opened wide. "Why wouldn't you? You bought your tickets already. I mean, unless you didn't have a da—" Willow stopped mid-sentence as Scott walked over toward the group. "Day or two to think it over," she added lamely, trying to cover quickly.

Cordelia's eyes darted from Buffy to Scott. "What's going on?" she demanded. "Scott hasn't asked her to the Homecoming dance yet?"

Suddenly all eyes were on Buffy and Scott. Buffy blushed slightly and took on an extremely uncomfortable visage. "Thank you, Cordelia. The humiliation's so good for my color."

Buffy wasn't the only one feeling uncomfortable. Scott shifted from foot to foot. "Oh," he gulped nervously. "I just sort of assumed that you'd think that was corny. But I'm in . . . you know, I mean if you want to."

"I do if you want to," Buffy agreed, just as nervously.

"I do," Scott assured her. "If you want to. . . ."

Buffy opened her mouth to speak, but Oz stopped her. "The judges will accept that as a 'yes,'" he joked, breaking the tension as only he could.

Both Buffy and Scott seemed relieved to have that over with. Cordelia was extremely impressed with herself. Buffy and Scott did make a good-looking couple.

Not as cute as her and Xander of course, but Buffy in her strapless zebra-print dress and Scott in his white shirt and black jacket did look pretty good together—in a monochromatic sort of way.

"You want another drink?' Scott asked Buffy.

Buffy shook her head. "You know what? I'm a little tired. Think I'll call it a night. I'm excited about the home-coming dance," she added, almost as an after thought. Then, before Scott could ask her any more questions, she leaned in and gave him a pretty nice public kiss.

But Buffy didn't go straight home after leaving the Bronze. Instead she headed to the edge of town, to an old abandoned mansion. She was on a mission, one she knew she had to keep secret even from her closest friends. Slowly she walked toward the French doors in the back of the giant old house. She was about to knock on the glass when the doors swung open.

There stood Angel, ready to attack.

"It's just me," Buffy said quietly, as she stared into his dark eyes. The only light in the room came from a fire burning in the hearth. Still, in the darkness, she could see Angel clearly, his smooth skin peeking out from his partially open shirt, his face filled with a suffering no one else could ever know.

Buffy bit her lip, thinking about all the pain Angel had caused her friends. It was why she hadn't yet told the other Scoobies that he'd been returned to the world—by some mysterious intervention even Buffy didn't quite comprehend. The Angel who had returned to her was different from the vamp she'd once loved so passionately. Although he was no longer on the hunt, he was more savage than before, almost animalistic.

Buffy was certain her friends would think she was crazy if they knew she was alone with him. And yet beneath the untamed exterior there were parts of him that were still the Angel she'd known.

Buffy *was* planning to tell her friends about Angel . . . eventually. But for now, it was just the two of them. Buffy handed the tortured vamp a package, a container of blood from the butcher shop. Angel grabbed it from her and sniffed at the plastic container, letting the smell of fresh blood fill his nose. Then he set it down on a table, unwilling to let Buffy see him sip the liquid.

"How are you feeling?" Buffy asked him nervously.

"It hurts . . . less," Angel replied quietly.

Buffy turned away for a second. It was so hard to see him like this. "I haven't told Giles and the others you're back," she told him finally.

"Giles," Angel said softly, remembering all he'd done to the librarian.

"I'm not going to. They wouldn't understand that you're"—Buffy hesitated a moment, unable to put words to her feelings— "better," she said finally.

Angel picked up the container of blood once again, but then thought better of it and set it back down. He was clearly agitated and upset.

"I'm going to help you keep getting better," Buffy assured him. She stopped for a moment, struggling with how she was going to tell Angel about her new life she'd put together in the months between when she'd killed him and when he'd returned. "It's just everything's different. I'm a senior now. I'm working harder at school, even thinking about college. Also, I'm involved with someone."

Buffy could see the words zap through him, like a stake through his heart. And yet Angel didn't say anything. He merely reached for her and fixed the twisted collar on her black leather jacket. Then he turned away again.

"His name is Scott," Buffy told him. "He's a nice solid guy. He makes me happy, and that's what I need: someone I can count on."

"I don't think we should see each other anymore."

Ouch! Insert knife and twist. Buffy stood in the school hallway the next morning, and stared at Scott with surprise and shock. Her eyes opened wide.

"You don't?" she asked, confused. "When did this happen? Where was I?"

Scott was clearly uncomfortable, but he forced himself to stay and explain. "Buffy, it's just before we were going out, you seemed so full of life, like a force of nature. Now you seem kind of distracted all the time and . . ."

Buffy knew what he meant. Ever since Angel had come back, she *had* been distracted. Her mind was with him. But she wanted to move on. "I'm getting better," she promised Scott. "And you're gonna be seeing a drastic distraction reduction from here on out." Buffy paused for minute, searching Scott's face for some sense of understanding, but there was nothing there. She forced herself to give a small laugh. "Drastic distraction reduction. Try saying that ten times fast."

"I'm really sorry," he assured her, as he walked away.

Buffy stood there, alone in the hall, watching him go. She felt very young and very alone. She could feel the tears forming in her eyes, and she was glad no one was around to see her this way.

But the truth was, someone was watching Buffy—from afar. At that very moment a van was parked outside the school. Inside was a high-tech surveillance setup, currently being monitored by two huge, muscular, Aryan types. The menacing twins were keeping a long-distance eye on her and, judging by the sadistic looks on their faces, enjoying their voyeurism. Frederick dialed up his cellular modem hookup and immediately transmitted Buffy's image to a computer in a mansion on the other side of town.

Inside the large stately home, a craggy old man rolled his wheelchair over toward his computer. He watched as Buffy's sad image flashed on his screen. "Is that her?" the old man asked his companion.

A tall, well-dressed African-American vamp with a sleek moustache and a gold hoop earring in each ear strolled over to the computer. A slight smile came over his lips as he looked at Buffy. "In the nubile flesh, my friend," Buffy's old vampire nemesis, Mr. Trick, assured the older man. "That's the target."

Buffy might not have known a thing about her stalkers, but the bigwigs at City Hall sure did. At that very moment, Deputy Mayor Allan Finch was in the Mayor's office reporting on his findings.

"I'm not sure how serious this is, but they were

spotted here three days ago." The Deputy Mayor placed two black-and-white snapshots on the Mayor's desk. "Their names are Frederick and Hans Gruenshtahler. Wanted in Europe for capital murder, terrorism, the bombing of Flight 1402, and—"

"Can I see your hands?" the Mayor interrupted him.

The deputy flinched. It was such an odd request. "Sir?"

"Your hands," said the Mayor, tapping on the blotter that sat on his large wooden desk.

The deputy mayor did as he was told, laying his hands out for inspection.

"I think these could be cleaner," the Mayor told him.

"I wash them," the deputy assured his boss.

"After every meal and under your fingernails. Dirt gets trapped there, and germs . . . and mayonnaise."

The deputy mayor stared at his employer nervously. He couldn't imagine what any of this had to do with the terrorists.

"My dear mother said cleanliness is next to godliness, and I believed her," the Mayor continued, speaking through his smile. Then he glanced at the pictures of Hans and Frederick. "I'd like these put under surveillance. And I'd like to know if any other colorful characters come to town," he added, bouncing back to the topic at hand.

The deputy mayor wasn't quite sure what had just happened, but he did know he had his orders—about his hands and Hans and Frederick.

"Absolutely," he assured the Mayor. "Thank you for your time."

While the politicians were discussing cleanliness and criminals, Willow and Xander were discussing a much more pressing topic—homecoming wear.

"You have to help me pick an outfit," Willow begged Xander as the two chums walked away from the makeshift yearbook-photo studio that had been set up in the school lounge. "I wanna wear something that'll make Oz go 'ooh.'"

"No problem," Xander agreed. "I got the tux goin' on. I'm gonna look hot . . . if it even remotely fits." He wandered over to where Cordelia was standing in the middle of the hall. She seemed totally entranced by what she was looking at. The problem was, Xander had absolutely no idea what that might be.

"Whatcha doin'?" he asked her playfully.

"Checking out the—I laughingly use the phrase— competition."

Xander smiled at Cordelia. She looked amazing in a simple sundress. He couldn't imagine her having any competition for anything.

Cordelia looked over at a small, smiling senior who was playing with her shoulder length brown hair and laughing with a crowd of kids. "Holly Charleston," she told Xander. "Nice girl, brain-dead. Doesn't have a prayer." She turned her attention to a tall leggy blonde who was dressed in a tight blue skirt and low-cut blouse. "Michelle Blake. Open to all mankind, especially if they have a letterman's jacket and a car." Cordelia considered that for a moment. "She could give me a run."

Oh, now Xander got it. Cordy was thinking about the Homecoming Queen contest . . . again.

Oz spotted his friends from across the room and strolled over toward them. It was obvious he hadn't put any extra thought into *his* senior picture—he had the same T-shirt and spiky hair look he always wore.

Willow smiled as her guy moved close to her. "Where's Buffy?" she asked the others. "She's going to miss the yearbook pictures."

Xander gave her a prurient grin. "She and Faith are in the library . . . getting sweaty."

"They're *training*," Cordelia corrected him.

"I stand by my phrase," Xander insisted.

"I don't think she was here the day they announced 'em," Oz recalled, bringing the conversation back to yearbook snapshots. "Did anybody tell her?"

"I'll tell her now," Cordelia volunteered. "I've gotta go by the Nurse's office for an ice pack anyway."

Xander's concern was plain. "Did you hurt yourself?"

"No, silly," Cordelia assured him. She patted her flawless face. "It shrinks the pores."

Slam! Buffy pounded a right hook into the pad Faith held in front of her. Then she switched to a left, and a right. She moved quickly and powerfully, so powerfully in fact that Faith winced every time Buffy's fist connected with the sparring pad.

"Man, guys should break up with you more often," Faith exclaimed in her tough Boston accent.

"Gee, thanks."

"No, I mean it," Faith assured her. "You got some quality rage going. Really gives you an edge."

Buffy frowned and and grabbed a towel. Quickly she wiped the sweat from her forehead and downed about half a bottle of Gatorade in one quick sip. "Edge girl. Just what I always wanted to be," she moaned.

Faith laughed slightly. "Well, screw him. You move on, you party—heavily—you'll be fine." She stopped and looked at her fellow slayer curiously. "You're still going to that dance, right?"

Buffy looked down at her sweat stained, purple spandex half shirt. Not exactly the type of look you'd expect from someone who was considering heading off to homecoming. "Maybe," she replied doubtfully.

"You got the tix already," Faith reminded her. "Why don't we go together?"

Buffy looked over at Faith's own work out outfit. She noticed a few drips of perspiration dripping from her forehead as well. *Wouldn't we make an attractive pair?* "I don't know about that," she said slowly.

"Come on," Faith urged. "We'll find a couple a studs, use 'em, and discard 'em. That's *always* fun."

Buffy considered the idea for a moment. "Okay," she agreed finally. "I'm in. Not the stud-using part—or probably not."

Cordelia passed by the library and peered in. Buffy and Faith were in the middle of some sort of heavy conversation. She was about to interrupt the Slayer-to-Slayer tête-à-tête to tell Buffy about the yearbook photos, when two familiar members of the football team passed by. Instantly Cordelia went into Homecoming Queen campaign mode.

"Bobby, Mashad," she greeted them, changing

direction to walk down the hall beside them. "Where's the love?"

That afternoon, after Buffy had showered and tried to wash all thoughts of Scott from her now carefully upswept hair, she wandered off into the quad, in search of Ms. Moran, her favorite teacher. She discovered the tall, pretty brunette walking toward her next class. Buffy hurried to catch up.

"Ms. Moran," she said sweetly as she fell in step with the teacher. "I'm so glad I ran into you." Ms. Moran stopped and looked at Buffy kindly—if with a bit of confusion.

"I had a little incident last year of getting kicked out of school," Buffy explained. "But I'm back now, I've done all my makeups, but I still need one written recommendation from a teacher—I think the word Principal Snyder used was 'glowing'—for my file, so I can prove I belong here."

Ms. Moran studied Buffy's face. "And you are. . . ?"

"Buffy. Buffy Summers." The name didn't seem to ring a bell with Ms. Moran. "Third row. I sat near the window," Buffy continued. "Contemporary American Heroes: From Amelia Earhart to Maya Angelou, the class that changed my life?"

"Were you absent a lot, uh. . . ?" Ms. Moran asked slowly.

"Buffy," she replied with a frown.

The next day, Buffy was in need of some serious support from her buds. She met up with them in the cafeteria, grateful for the opportunity to unload on someone.

"I can't believe it," Buffy moaned. "My favorite teacher and she didn't even know who I was. I'm like a non-person. Am I invisible?" She turned to Oz. "Can you see me?

"Big as life," Oz assured her.

"At Hemery I was Prom Queen, Fiesta Queen, I was on the cheerleading squad. The yearbook was like the story of me." Buffy recalled, her face lighting up just at the thought of the normal, popular life she'd had at her Los Angeles school. "Now it's senior year and I'm gonna be one crappy picture on one eighth of one crappy page."

Xander cringed. "Uh, no. Actually you're not."

"What do you mean?" Buffy asked suspiciously.

"Well, you missed the picture taking."

There was no missing the shock on Buffy's face. "When? Why?"

"We did 'em yesterday," Oz explained.

"Didn't Cordelia tell you?" Willow added.

All eyes turned to the other side of the cafeteria, where Cordelia was handing out flyers, and urging students to give her their vote in the Homecoming Queen competition. Before anyone could try and stop her, Buffy leaped up from the table and strode purposefully over toward Cordelia.

"Buffy," Cordy greeted her with surprise. "You look adorable in that outfit." It was obvious from the fake smile and the look of disdain in her eyes that Buffy's cardigan and sundress were not really Cordelia's idea of adorable.

"I'm not voting for you," Buffy snapped back, well aware of Cordelia's talent for fake compliments.

Cordelia rolled her eyes. "Then make it snappy."

"Why didn't you tell me they were doing the yearbook pictures?"

Cordelia shrugged. "Didn't I? I guess I forgot. What's the big?"

"You just could have thought about someone else for thirty seconds," Buffy informed her angrily. "That's all."

Cordelia seemed surprise at Buffy's anger. "Hey, I'm under a lot of pressure here," she explained.

"Oh, yeah, homecoming campaign," Buffy snapped back sarcastically. "Rough gig."

"What would you know about it? Just because you were Guacamole Queen when you were three doesn't mean you understand how it works."

Buffy looked down at the eight-by-ten color photos Cordelia was giving to passersby. "Obviously it involves handing out these entirely lame flyers."

"No. It involves being a part of the school and having actual friends," Cordelia informed Buffy angrily. "Now if it was about monsters, blood, and innards, you'd be a shoo-in."

From the look of total furor and pain that came over Buffy's face, it was obvious that Cordelia had gone too far. But Cordy was on a roll, and she wasn't about to stop now. "Like to see you try to win the crown," the brunette added as she turned to walk away.

Buffy's green eyes turned to steel. "Then you will."

Cordelia turned back and glowered at Buffy. "What does that mean?"

"I'll show you how it's done," Buffy informed her. "I'm going to go for Homecoming Queen, and I'm going to win."

Cordelia made no attempt to choke back her sense of amusement with Buffy's declaration. "This is starting to be sad."

"Sorry, Cordy, but you have no idea who you're messing with."

Cordelia all but laughed in Buffy's face. "What? The Slayer?"

But Buffy wasn't laughing. She was dead serious. "I'm not talking about the Slayer. I'm talking about Buffy," she informed her rival. "You've awakened the prom queen within, Cordy. And that crown is gonna be mine."

Mr. Trick strutted around the drawing room of the old man's mansion with a confident sense of purpose. As always the vamp was impeccably groomed and in total control of his unholy assembly: The old man, Frederick and Hans, a Texas vampire cowboy and his undead bride, a big-game hunter, and a bizarre-looking demon with spikes on his head.

"Competition is a beautiful thing," Trick informed the assorted sordid killers. "Makes us strive. Makes us accomplish. Occasionally makes us kill. We all feel the desire to win, whether we're human, vampire, or . . ." The well-dressed vamp stopped and stared at the tall, muscular, yellow-faced, spiked-headed monster. "Or whatever the hell you are, my brother. Got them spiny-looking head things. I never seen that."

The monster stood tall and proud of heritage. "I am Kulak of the Miquot clan."

"Isn't that nice," Mr. Trick murmured. "Point is,

you're all here for the same reason."

"Well, it wasn't for no philosophy class," the cowboy vampire joked.

Mr. Trick was not a vamp who suffered fools lightly. And he was in no mood for jokes. "Mr. Gorch," he said, his voice dripping with venom, "my account statement says your deposit has yet to be made."

Lyle Gorch reached into his pocket and dumped a sack full of blood-stained hundred-dollar bills on the table. "Me and Candy's blowing our whole honeymoon stash on this little game."

Mr. Trick looked at the bloody bills and grimaced. "They're dirty," he complained.

Lyle smiled, revealing his disgustingly rotting teeth. "They're nonconsecutive."

Apparently this little piece of information satisfied Mr. Trick, because he continued talking. "In a few days' time, the game will commence," he told the group. "You will all have the opportunity to bring down not one, but *two* of the toughest prize bucks this world has to offer. The first target, Buffy, you've all seen. The second, Faith, is more elusive, but both targets will be together and ready for the killing, and that's a money-back guarantee.

"Ladies, gentlemen, and spiny-headed lookin' creatures, welcome to Slayerfest '98."

Buffy and Cordelia's minds were focused on the Homecoming Queen competition, and Mr. Trick's mind was on the Slayerfest, but Willow and Xander could think of only the dance. At the moment, they were both in Willow's room, trying to come up with just the right look for the big night. Xander was making sure his tux fit. Willow was searching her closet for an appropriate outfit. Finally she stepped out from behind a large white screen at the edge of her room and modeled a red silk blouse for Xander. "What do you think of this?"

"Nice," Xander murmured. He didn't sound too enthused.

Willow got the picture. She began to rummage through the pile of clothes on her bed for something else. "It's my first big dance," she explained to Xander as she changed discretely behind the screen. "You know, where there's a boy and a band and not just me alone in my room *pretending* there's a boy and a band. I want it to be . . ."

"Special," Xander finished her thought. "Which is why I spared no expense on the tux."

"The tux?" Willow asked. "I thought you borrowed that from your cousin Rigby."

"Expense to my *pride*, Will," Xander admitted, as he struggled to fix his bow tie. "They're our only relations with money and they shun us. As they should," he added.

Willow came out from behind the screen and shyly modeled a long floral skirt with a matching black top. "What do you think of this?"

Xander gave her another noncommittal "nice," and then went back to struggling with his tie.

Willow nodded. She wasn't crazy about the outfit either. She reached over and tied Xander's bow tie for him. Then she started to giggle.

"What?" Xander demanded.

"I was just . . . remember the eighth-grade cotillion?" Willow asked. "You had that clip-on . . ."

"I was stylin' with that clip-on."

"And now here we are," Willow mused. "It's home-coming."

"We should face it, Will. You and I are gonna be in neighboring rest homes," Xander told her. "And I'm gonna be stopping by to have you adjust my . . . my . . . I can't think of anything that's not really gross."

Willow gave him a quick smile. Then she picked up another outfit from the bed and disappeared behind the screen once more.

"So, uh, you and Oz," Xander began casually as he buttoned his black vest. "How can I put this? Are we on first, second, or . . . yee gods!"

"That is none of your business, Alexander Harris!"

"Oh," Xander declared, sounding more than a little impressed. "Rounding second."

"You don't know that," Willow countered. "How about you and Cordelia?"

Xander slipped on his tux jacket. "A gentleman never talks about his conquests."

"Since when did you become a gentleman?" Willow teased. She stepped out from behind the screen and modeled her newest choice, a slinky black evening gown.

Xander stared at her for a very long moment. So long that Willow became uncomfortable. She looked down and smoothed the silky black fabric. "I know. 'Nice,'" Willow said.

"I was gonna go with 'gorgeous,'" Xander corrected her.

Willow smiled shyly. "Really?"

Xander nodded, but said nothing.

"You too," Willow told him. Then she added quickly. "In a guy way."

"Oz is very lucky," Xander assured his best friend.

"So is Cordelia," Willow said. "In a girl way."

That was it. For the first time in their whole lives, they didn't know what to say to each other. Finally it was Willow who broke the uncomfortable silence.

"I don't know if I can dance in this." She thought for a second, a touch of panic rising into her face. "I don't know if I can *dance*."

"Piece of cake," Xander assured her. He reached out his hand. "Here."

Slowly Willow took his hand, and they began a slow, uncomfortable dance. But as they moved across the carpeted floor in Willow's room, the two friends relaxed. Without even realizing what they were doing, they moved their bodies closer, and closer. Touching. And then . . . they kissed—gently at first, and then with the sort of passion that's usually reserved for boyfriend-and-girlfriend type relationships. The kiss lasted only a few seconds before both Willow and Xander leaped away from one another.

"That didn't just happen," Xander insisted nervously.

"No," Willow agreed quickly. "I mean it did. But it didn't."

"Because I respect you," Xander assured her, "*and* Oz, and I would never . . ."

"I wouldn't ever either," Willow interrupted. "It must be the clothes. It's a fluke."

"It's a clothes fluke," Xander agreed. "And that's what it is and there'll *be* no more fluking!"

"Not ever," Willow agreed. She looked up at him. He stared at her. And for a moment, it seemed as though there could be a lot *more* fluking.

"We got to get out of these clothes!" Xander insisted.

"Right now!" Willow agreed.

Xander blushed red, realizing how that must have sounded. "Oh, I didn't mean . . ."

"Me either," Willow answered breathlessly as she disappeared behind the screen.

The next day, Willow and Xander sat as far from each other as possible when the Scooby Squad gathered in the library for a strategy meeting. This meeting was different, however, because they weren't getting together to discuss stakes or high kicks or cemeteries. They were there to begin Buffy's battle to take over the homecoming crown.

"A campaign is like a war," Buffy told the others. "It's won or lost in the trenches." She pointed to a huge white board behind her. The board was covered with pictures of Buffy's competition, as well as lists of each of their pros and cons. "Holly, Michelle, and our real competition, Cordelia, all have a big head start." She paused for a second and smiled at her assembled warriors. "Speaking of Cordelia's head, if I had a watermelon that big, I'd be rich."

Willow, Oz, and Xander stared at her blankly.

"Waits for laugh," Buffy joked. None came. So

Buffy continued her speech. "Right, don't rag on the competition. Makes me look petty." Buffy faced her friends. Still no reaction. Now she began to babble nervously as she thought out loud. "This is just like any popularity contest; I've done this before. The only difference being this time I'm not actually popular. But I'm not unpopular exactly. I mean a lot of people came to my welcome-home party."

"But they were killed by zombies," Willow reminded her.

The girl had a point. This was not going to be like any other popularity contest she'd ever been a part of—and Cordelia was probably the toughest foe she'd ever faced, in a homecoming queen situation anyway. "Willow, I want you to set up a database: who's for us, who's on the fence, where our real crisis areas are." Buffy turned to Oz. "You take the fringe, musicians not inclined to vote. Xander—" She stopped speaking and followed her friends' eyes, all of which were leading to the library door.

That's where Cordelia stood, dressed in full battle gear—white sleeveless turtleneck, short gray pleated skirt, and a matching gray-and-white handbag.

"Hi, Cordelia," Buffy greeted her. "I know this is a little awkward, but I don't see any reason why we can't all get along during the campaign. We're almost friends, and we're all going to the dance together in the limo."

"Great," Cordelia agreed. She turned to Willow. "How's the database coming?"

The guilt was clearly present in Willow's eyes as

she tried desperately to avoid Buffy's surprised gaze. "Uh, it's just about done."

Cordelia nodded. "Xander?"

"I've got your new flyers," he assured her.

Cordelia smiled triumphantly. "Let's get cracking," she told the others as she headed toward the door.

Xander looked helplessly at Buffy. "She's my girlfriend," he explained.

"It's just . . . she needs it so much more than you do." Willow tried to justify her actions.

Oz had a more direct rationalization. "As Willow goes, so goes my nation," he offered weakly.

Buffy couldn't say anything. She stood there in total shock, abandoned by her closest allies.

Cordelia smiled triumphantly. "Thanks for what you said, Buffy. I think we're getting along good, don't you?"

As Cordy turned to leave, Buffy stood by herself for a moment, contemplating what had just happened. Her friends had all just abandoned her—for Cordelia of all people. Well, not *all* her friends. Giles was still there, quietly shelving books in the library.

"Seems an awful fuss for a little title," he remarked, perching himself on a nearby desk.

"It's no fun if you don't try your best," Buffy countered.

Giles nodded slowly. "As long as fun is still in the mix."

Buffy smiled and picked up a bottle of Snapple. She took a long sip. "Sure. It's not like anyone takes it that seriously." She would have sounded believable, too—

had she not squeezed the bottle so hard that the glass shattered in her hand.

If her friends' defection had any effect on Buffy, it was to strengthen her resolve to win. After all, she figured if you wanted something done right, you had to do it yourself. And that meant that Buffy had only a few days to get really popular—really fast. *More queen, less Slayer.* She found that powder blue in particular brought out her eyes. She also started making cupcakes and hanging posters. And if some of those Buffy Summers posters just happened to land right on top of Cordelia's, so much the better.

Cordelia wasn't taking any of this lying down. While Buffy was handing out cupcakes, she was dispensing dessert baskets. And for every poster Buffy displayed, Cordelia added two of her own.

Buffy was surprised just how exhausting the whole meet-and-greet process was. She'd spent half the day talking baseball with the jocks and science theories with the nerds (not that either of those were topics that came easily to her), and she was almost as worn out as she was after a night of vampire slaying. She didn't remember being this tired during her campaigns back in Los Angeles. Still, Buffy wasn't discouraged. She figured that running for Homecoming Queen was like anything else—she just had to build up her campaigning endurance. She looked over at one of Cordelia's posters on the wall. It read GET MORE WITH COR. Buffy gleefully changed the saying to "Get Bored with Cor." Then she turned and prepared to hand out some of her own flyers to the kids passing by in the quad.

She wasn't out there two minutes, however, when she somehow managed to drop the entire pile of flyers. As she wearily stooped down to pick them up, Scott passed by. He bent down and lent his ex a hand.

"Here," he said kindly.

"Oh. Thanks," Buffy replied awkwardly.

Scott looked at the flyer. "I heard you were doing this."

Suddenly Buffy felt embarrassed. "It's just something to pass the time. Kind of silly really."

"I don't think so," Scott replied. His large, earnest eyes stared into Buffy's. "For what it's worth, you've got my vote."

"I really don't want you to feel that—" Buffy began. She caught herself mid-sentence. "Thank you." She looked at him with just a touch of wistfulness in her eyes.

Scott nodded a little self-consciously and walked off. As soon as he was out of sight, Buffy dropped her sad little girl act and whipped out her notebook. A list of every senior at Sunnydale High filled the pages. Some kids' names were crossed off, others had check marks beside them, and still others were blank, meaning Buffy still had a shot at swinging their vote her way. A broad smile passed over her lips as she put a check mark next Scott's name.

As she wandered into the lounge in search of more students to seduce into voting for her, Buffy spotted Willow staring at her campaign posters as well Cordelia's. Will looked positively guilt-ridden. Buffy smiled to herself. That was exactly what she'd been counting on.

"Hi," Buffy greeted Will.

"Oh, hi. How are you. You good? You look good. And what else is new with you? Did I mention you look good?" Willow was jabbering at top speed, not even breathing between words.

"Will, it's okay, you helping Cordelia," Buffy assured her. "We're best friends. I'm not going to hold it against you."

Willow shook her head adamantly. "No. I'm not a friend. I'm a rabid dog who should be shot. But there are forces at work here. Dark, incomprehensible forces."

"And I'm sure they're more important than all we've been through together, or the number of times I've saved your life . . ."

"What do you want?" Willow's voice was painfully small now.

Buffy smiled triumphantly. "Fifteen minutes alone on your computer with Cordelia's data base."

"'Kay," Willow agreed, in an even tinier voice.

Buffy put her arm around Willow and steered her out of the lounge. "So I called the limo place and we're all set," Buffy told Willow. She sounded quite chipper now. "It's gonna swing by Faith, then me, then your house, unless you're gonna be at Oz's, and then . . ."

Willow listened without saying much. She was too guilt-ridden to talk. Guilt-ridden about Xander, about helping Cordelia, and about letting Buffy take a peek into Cordy's private prom database.

Back in the dark mansion at the edge of the town, the

old man taking part in Mr. Trick's Slayerfest was busy running map grids of Sunnydale on his PC. And he wasn't the only one preparing for the Fest. Frederick and Hans were involved in some heavy duty hand-to-hand sparring practice, and Kulak, the spiky-headed monster, was inspecting the blades on the knives that were implanted in his scaly forearms. Frawley, the big-game hunter, was checking the action on his massive rifle. Only Lyle Gorch and his new wife Candy seemed oblivious to the need for planning. They were busy necking, as only two vamps in love could.

But Buffy was blissfully unaware of the goings on across town. As far as she knew, the only enemy she had to face was a brunette with a frighteningly toothsome smile. And at this very moment, that dangerous creature was busy flirting with a group of extreme science nerds.

"Are you kidding?" Cordelia asked with mock indignation. "I've been doing the Vulcan death grip since I was four!" She reached out her hand and touched the arm of one of the Star Trek freaks.

Buffy wasn't doing any better. She'd just handed a senior named Jonathan a big, creamy chocolate cupcake. "You know, Jonathan," she said with a smile, "I've always felt a special bond between you and me."

But Jonathan wasn't falling for her line. "Cordelia gave me six bucks," he informed Buffy as he took a bite of the creamy frosting. "That buys a whole lot of cupcakes."

Buffy's green eyes flashed. "Okay, how about you

vote for me, and I don't beat the living crap out of you?"

One look at Buffy's deadpan expression was all it took for Jonathan to see things her way.

Once she'd secured Jonathan's vote, Buffy strutted angrily over to confront Cordelia. "You're giving out money now?

"So?" Cordelia asked innocently. "Is that any more tacky than your 'I'm a shy but deep girl' posters?"

"Yes," Buffy insisted.

Cordelia looked bored. "This whole trying to be like me really isn't funny any more."

Now Buffy was really angry. "I was never trying to be like you," she assured Cordelia. "And when was it funny?"

"I don't see why your pathetic need to recapture your glory days gives you the right to splinter my vote!" Cordy barked.

Buffy looked at her incredulously. "How can you think it's okay to talk to people like this?" she demanded. "Do you have parents?"

"Yeah, two of them," Cordelia shot back. "Unlike some people."

The barb met its mark. Buffy felt as though she'd been slapped across the face. "Your brain isn't even connected to your mouth, is it?" she spat out.

"Why don't you do us both a favor and stay out of my way," Cordelia said, effectively closing the conversation as she tried to walk past Buffy.

But Buffy wasn't having any of that. She caught Cordelia by the hand and held her firmly in place.

"Don't ever do that again," Buffy warned, enunciating each word so that there would be no mistaking the menace in her voice.

"You're sick, you know that?" Cordelia accused.

Just then Xander and Willow hurried over. Xander grabbed his girlfriend before anything more violent could happen. "Okay, let's not say things we'll regret later," he said.

"Crazy freak!" Cordelia barked at Buffy.

"Vapid whore!" Buffy thundered back.

Xander cringed. "Like that," he interrupted.

But Cordelia was beyond listening to anyone. "What did you call me?" she demanded of Buffy.

Before Buffy could reply, Xander pulled Cordelia away. Willow stood beside Buffy, frowning as she watched Xander and Cordelia walk off. Things had gotten really out of hand.

Late that afternoon, Xander and Willow met up at her house. They were both totally wigged out by the past twenty-four hours.

"This is just the worst thing that's ever happened," Willow moaned.

"I know, I know," Xander agreed, putting his hands on her shoulders, "but when I look at you now, it's like I'm seeing you for the first time."

"I was talking about Buffy and Cordelia."

Xander immediately dropped his hands from her body. "Me too," he said sheepishly.

"What are we gonna do?" Willow asked him. "We have to do something. This all our fault."

Xander looked at Willow with amazement. Somehow she always seemed to take the world's problems on as her own. And her shoulders were much too small for a heavy load like that. "How do you get from chick fight to 'our fault'?" he asked her.

"Because we felt so guilty about the fluke that we overcompensated by helping Cordelia and spun the whole group dynamic out of orbit." She stopped for a minute to catch her breath. "We're a meteor storm heading for Earth."

"Calm down, calm down. Let's put our heads together and think of something," he suggested. "One of us is pretty darn smart and I'm"—he paused for an instant and frowned— "I'm just in hell. I thought being a senior—at last—and having a girlfriend—at last—would be a good thing. Why wouldn't that be a good thing?"

Willow looked at him and grinned with amusement.

"What?" he demanded.

"Sometimes when you're falling apart, your mouth does the sweetest thing," she told him.

Xander scanned her face gently. "My mouth?"

Willow reached over and placed her fingers on his lips. Quietly Xander touched her hand. They sat that way for a moment, afraid to move. Finally Willow pulled away.

"What are we gonna do?" she asked Xander.

"We just gotta get the two of them communicating," Xander suggested.

Willow shook her head. "I'm talking about us."

• • •

When the night of the homecoming dance finally arrived, Buffy was ready. There was no way she was going to fade into the background on this evening. She was done up bright red—from the spaghetti straps of her satin three quarter length gown, to the tips of her stilettos. Her upswept do and dangling earrings added just enough class. So when the long, black stretch limo stopped at her house, she felt every bit like the homecoming royalty she was sure—or okay, *pretty* sure—she was about to become.

Cordelia was also dressed for prom queen success, in a green satin clingy number with a slit all the way up the side, that must have cost a fortune. As she stepped into the limo, Buffy looked at her peculiarly. According to the plan Buffy had worked out earlier, Cordelia would be the *last* picked up, not the first.

"What are you doing here? Where's Faith?" Buffy demanded.

Cordelia refused to answer, never mind look in Buffy's direction. Instead she handed Buffy an envelope.

Buffy pulled the thin white slip of paper from the envelope and read the note aloud. "Dear Cordelia and Buffy. We won't be riding to the dance with you. We want you to work out your problems because our friendships are more important than who wins Homecoming Queen. Your Friends. P.S.: The limo was not cheap. Work it out."

Buffy sighed. This was not good. She looked down at the seat between Cordelia and herself. There were two corsage boxes. One was empty. "They bought us corsages?" Buffy wondered.

"I took the orchid," Cordelia informed her.

Buffy frowned slightly as she struggled to keep her temper in check. "Okay," she muttered as she pinned the other flower to her dress. "Nice of you to check with me on that."

Cordelia shot her a look that could only be construed as pure evil. "I don't see what the big deal is."

"I'm not making a big deal," Buffy insisted. "You wanted the orchid, you got the orchid."

"It goes with my complexion better."

Buffy studied Cordelia's face. "It does have that sallow tint," she noted sarcastically.

Suddenly the limo stopped. The driver's door opened. "Finally, we're here," Buffy noted. She waited for the driver to come around and open the door for her, but he never arrived. Instead she heard his heavy footsteps run off into the night. Buffy opened her door, stepped out of the limo, and looked around. They were definitely not anywhere near the dance. The car had stopped in the middle of the woods—in the middle of *nowhere*.

"What is this?" Cordelia asked as she got out of the car. "Okay, guys, we've had enough of your stupid games," she called out into the trees.

But no one answered.

Buffy's intuition was telling her that this was no friendly joke being played on the girls. This was trouble. "What's massively wrong with this picture?" she wondered aloud. As she turned her head, Buffy noticed a huge screen TV sitting alone at the edge of the woods. She walked toward the set. Cordelia followed close behind, suddenly not anxious to be alone.

Attached to the TV was a note that read simply, "PRESS PLAY." Buffy did as she was told. Immediately Mr. Trick's smooth, suave visage appeared on the screen.

"Hello, ladies," Mr. Trick said. "Welcome to Slayerfest '98. What is a slayerfest you ask? Well, as in most of life, there's the hunters and the hunted. Can you guess where you two fall? From the beginning of this tape you have exactly thirty seconds"—the taped image of Mr. Trick looked down at his watch— "oooh, seventeen now, to run for your lives. Faith, Buffy, have a nice death."

Buffy turned around, rapidly scanning the woods for potential killers. Cordelia however, continued staring at the screen, yelling at the taped image. "Hello. How stupid are you people? She's a slayer. I am a homecoming quee—"

Before Cordelia could finish her diatribe, a loud shot rang out in the darkness. The bullet shattered the TV, blowing it to bits. Quickly Buffy grabbed Cordelia and pulled her into the woods.

If Slayerfest was no fest for Buffy and Cordelia, homecoming was not exactly a joy either. At least not for Xander and Willow. They were spending the evening at the Bronze trying to keep their distance from one another. Basically they were just standing around, moping to the music being played by Oz's band.

Faith, decked out in a black clingy number that revealed her arm-band tattoo and a lot more, wandered over toward the morose duo. "What are you two so mopey about?" she asked them.

"We're not mopey," Xander disagreed rather unconvincingly. "We're grooving on Oz's band. He's a wonderful guy, Oz."

"He wrote this song for me," Willow added, her eyes welling up with tears.

Faith turned her head slightly, just in time to see Buffy's ex gliding by with his date. "That sleazebag," she declared angrily. She wandered off in Scott's direction.

Willow and Xander went back to standing around listening unenthusiastically to Oz's band. Giles spotted them from across the room. "We've got to find Buffy! Something terrible's happened!"

That knocked Xander and Willow right out of their funk. Their bodies tensed, and their eyes grew worried with concern.

Giles started to laugh. "Just kidding! Thought I'd give you a scare." He looked over at the small sandwich Xander was nibbling on. "Are those finger sandwiches?"

Willow and Xander looked at each other with surprise. This night was so bizarre. Not only did they have this whole fluke thing to worry about, but now Giles had seemed to have developed a sense of humor. Could things get any weirder?

As Buffy and Cordelia ran through the woods— in heels, no less—they were constantly on the look out for . . . well, Buffy wasn't quite sure what they were looking for, since she had no clue who was actually after them.

"I have an idea," Cordelia suggested as they moved swiftly through the dark trees. "We talk to these people, we explain I'm not a slayer, they let me go . . . LOOK OUT!" Cordelia pointed to Buffy's foot which was just about to step into a well-hidden bear trap. Quickly Buffy lifted her foot, just moments before the trap snapped shut.

At the sound of the snap, Frawley, the big game hunter, emerged from the dark woods. His gun was at the ready and aimed straight at Buffy's heart. Without a moment's hesitation, Buffy bent down, picked up the trap, and whirled it straight for him. The trap slammed into Frawley's head. He dropped his gun and staggered backwards.

Snap. Caught by another of his own traps.

"That's gotta smart," Buffy remarked as she grabbed Frawley's gun from the ground and aimed it at him. "Now, I can let you out of that trap, or I can put a bullet in your head. How many are there in this little game and what are they packing?"

For a minute Frawley said nothing. He wasn't at all sure that this little blonde was really going to shoot him, even if she was a slayer. But as soon as Buffy worked the action on his rifle, Frawley knew she meant business.

"There's me, two Germans with AR-15s and a grenade launcher, yellow-skinned demon with long knives, vampire couple from Texas named Gorch," he said, barely taking a breath between words.

"That everybody?" Buffy demanded.

"Everybody who's out here," Frawley assured her. "Germans are wired. Their boss is tracking them on computer. Now get me out of this!"

Cordelia looked pleadingly at Frawley. "Could you do me an eensy favor," she asked him. "Tell your friends that I'm not—"

Before Cordy could reveal the truth about herself, Buffy slapped her hand over the girl's mouth to keep her quiet. Then, sensing danger, she spun around—and came face-to-face with a spiky yellow monster. Kulak whipped his sharp blade in Buffy's direction. Buffy shot off the rifle. Kulak's aim was bad, and the blade missed its mark. Buffy's shot fared better, knocking Kulak backward and to the ground, shocking him, but not killing him.

Cordelia let out a scream. Quickly Buffy grabbed her and pulled her away from the scene. She didn't want to be around when that monster came to.

Just as Buffy was hell-bent on protecting Cordelia (not to mention her own hide), Faith was being, well, *faithful*, to her friend Buffy. She slithered over toward Scott and his date, and came right between them on the dance floor.

"Scott, there you are honey," she greeted him in a voice just dripping with familiarity. "Good news. The doctor says the itching, the swelling, and the burning should clear up, but we gotta keep using the ointment." She turned to his date and smiled sweetly. "Hi," she said, as she danced away smiling to herself.

Xander and Willow, however, hadn't cracked a

smile all night. In fact, they were still staring blindly at the stage, afraid to look at each other.

"I suspect these finger foods contain actual finger," Giles remarked as he walked over to them after a failed visit to the refreshment table. "I think I'll retreat to the library until the coronation. I want to be here when Buffy . . . however the thing turns out for her." He stopped for a moment and smiled proudly at Willow and Xander. "That was a fine thing you two did, putting Buffy and Cordelia together."

As Giles walked off, Willow frowned. "We did one fine thing."

"Yeah," Xander agreed with an equal lack of enthusiasm. "They've been gone a while. They must be really getting into it."

But the only thing Buffy and Cordelia were getting into at the moment was a deserted cabin they'd discovered deep in the woods. The place was old and rotting, with just a few pieces of broken furniture lying around, but it would provide shelter for a while, at least until Buffy could figure out a plan of action. The Slayer slammed the door and wedged an old chair under the door handle. Then she looked around. "We're safe, for the time being," she told Cordelia as she closed the shutters on one of the windows. "Look for a weapon."

Cordelia watched as a termite-infested shutter came off in Buffy's hands, leaving another of the cabin's glass windows in plain view. Suddenly Cordy had to struggle to catch her breath. "Safe?" she cried out. "I'm not safe. I'm going to die."

"You are if you just stand there," Buffy informed her.

"I'm never going to be crowned Homecoming Queen. I'm never going to graduate from high school. I'm never going to know if it was real between me and Xander or some temporary insanity that made me think . . . I loved him." She paused for a second, realizing the incredible weight of her emotions. Then she started to cry. "And now I'll never get to tell him."

Buffy took a deep breath. "Yes, you are," she told Cordelia firmly. "We're going to get out of here. Then we're going to the library where Giles and the rest of the weapons live, and we're gonna take the rest of those creeps out in time for you to congratulate me on my sweeping victory as Homecoming Queen."

Cordelia gave Buffy a knowing stare. "I know what you're up to," she told her. "You think if you can get me mad enough, I won't be so scared." She paused for a minute. "Hey, it's working!" she admitted as she ran over to an old chest of drawers and began ransacking the furniture. "Where's a damn weapon?" she shouted.

Buffy stood by the open window, her gun at the ready. "Do you really love Xander?"

"Well," Cordelia began, as she opened another old drawer, "he just grows on you, like a Chia Pet." She stood and joined Buffy at the window, weapon in hand.

Buffy stared at Cordelia. The brunette was wielding a wooden spatula. "That's it?" she asked.

"Just this and a telephone," Cordelia answered.

Buffy stared at her, incredulous. "A telephone? You didn't think a telephone would be helpful?"

Cordelia began to move her spatula up and down, as though she were beating an invisible bad guy on the head. "This is better for . . . oh," she added, realizing what Buffy had meant. Quickly Buffy grabbed the phone from Cordy's hand and began to dial.

● ● ●

As the Slayer punched in Giles phone number, the old man in the mansion was busy inputting some numbers of his own into his computer, trying to track Buffy and Cordelia. Mr. Trick stood by his side, munching on a big bowl of popcorn, as though he were watching an action flick on TV.

"You're about to see why Daniel Boone and that idiot demon are creatures of the past, and why I'm the future," the old man informed Trick. He stopped suddenly and stared at the monitor. "I'm picking up a signal. They've got a phone!" The old man and the vampire excitedly eavesdropped on Buffy's frantic call.

"If you get this message, get help," Buffy told the librarian's answering machine. "Get out here—" Suddenly there was a click on the line.

"What happened?" Cordelia asked, as Buffy dropped the phone from her ear.

"It just went dead," Buffy said in a flat, eerily-calm voice. She stared out the window into the dark night. Her enemies were out there somewhere, that Buffy knew for sure. What she didn't know was when or where they might attack next.

Cordelia sat on a rickety old chair and clung to her spatula. "Why is it every time I go somewhere with you, it always ends in violence and terror?" she moaned to Buffy.

"Welcome to my life."

"I don't want to be in your life," Cordelia insisted. "I want to be in *my* life."

"Well, there's the door," Buffy replied. "Please feel free to leave at any time and live your life."

But her sarcasm was lost on Cordelia. The cheerleader was too far into self-pity mode to hear much of anything else. "All I wanted was to be Homecoming Queen," she continued.

"Well, that's all I wanted too, Cordelia." Buffy looked ruefully at her red-hot crimson dress. It was stained and slightly torn. "I spent a year's allowance on this dress."

"I don't get why you even care about homecoming when you're doing stuff like this," Cordelia interrupted.

"Because this is all I do. This is what my life is," Buffy explained. She grew quiet for a minute, trying to get her thoughts in order, trying to make Cordelia see why this had all been so important. "I thought, Homecoming Queen. I could pick up a yearbook someday and say, 'I was there. I went to high school, I had friends,' and for one moment there'd be proof. Proof that I was chosen for something other than this." She lifted the rifle in the air and pumped a shell into it. "Besides, I look cute in a tiara."

Suddenly there was a rustling in the leaves outside. "Do you hear—" Cordelia began, but she didn't get to finish her sentence. She was drowned out by the wild, animal-like screams of Kulak as the spiny-headed monster leaped through the shuttered window. Glass splintered everywhere, but Kulak seemed unharmed. He dove for Buffy and rammed her to the ground, knocking her rifle from her hands. But Buffy was quick. She leaped to her feet, yanked an old pair of deer antlers from the wall, and began to swing the headless horns in the air.

Unfortunately the antlers were no match for the crazed monster. Neither, for that matter, was a spatula—which Cordelia was slamming over Kulak's head again and again. The cooking utensil didn't even make a dent in his spikes.

But the rifle was still on the floor. From her angle, Buffy couldn't dive for it—but Cordelia could. "Cor . . . the gun!" Buffy ordered. Cordelia did as she was told. She bent down, lifted the gun . . . and then couldn't figure out how to work it. Finally she managed to get her finger on the trigger and with a loud bang, was able to get a shot off. The bullet soared over Buffy's head, managing to shatter an old whisky bottle sitting on a shelf.

Obviously Cordelia and a rifle were not a good match.

"Cordelia, the spatula," Buffy ordered as she ducked to avoid one of Kulak's flying blades. Then she leaped up in the air, grabbed onto an old wooden chandelier, and swung through the air, kicking the monster right in the face. She came to a landing right beside the rifle. Quickly she aimed the gun and pulled the trigger. But nothing happened. Cordelia had shot the last bullet.

Kulak grinned triumphantly. But before he could

complete his kill, a small metal object crashed through the glass window of the cabin.

A grenade. Obviously someone else beside Kulak knew where the girls had been hiding. Quickly Buffy grabbed Cordelia by the waist, and the two girls leaped through an open window. Kulak tried to leap through the other window, but the shutters held fast. The monster landed with a thud on the floor of the cabin. He had just enough time to stare at the grenade before . . . KABOOM!

Bye-bye, monster.

Buffy and Cordelia watched as the cabin exploded into a volcanic inferno. There was only one thing to do. "We gotta get to the library," Buffy told Cordelia.

The girls ran off, completely unaware that Frederick and Hans were close behind, ear pieces in place. The muscular, maniacal twins were awaiting their next order from the old man with the computer. Their grenade may not have killed the slayers, but the brothers were determined that their next move would do the job.

By now Cordelia and Buffy had crossed paths with a hunter, a monster, and two Aryan psychos. But they had yet to meet the other participants in Mr. Trick's sick game, Lyle and Candy Gorch. That was because the honeymooning vamps were nowhere near the woods. They'd moved the Slayerfest to a whole new location: the library of Sunnydale High.

Candy stood by a stack of books and absentmindedly pulled back on a crossbow as she waited impatiently for the action to begin. When the point of the bow moved a little too close to his heart, Lyle pushed it aside. He had no intention of meeting an untimely demise at the hands of the vamp of his dreams. "Easy darlin'," he warned her gently. "Those things'll go through ya quicker 'n' Grampa Pete's chili."

Candy moved the crossbow away. "I want to do Buffy," she whined. Then she looked at her new husband with a little-girl pout. "My weddin' present fer what happened to your poor brother. When's she coming?"

Lyle gave his wife a reassuring glance. He hadn't forgotten that Buffy had been the one to slay his brother. And he was every bit as determined as Candy to see the Slayer fall.

As he looked down at the floor, where Giles now lay, unconscious with a huge bruise on his head, Lyle knew it wouldn't be long now.

"He's her Watcher. She'll show," Lyle assured his wife. "As soon as she takes out some of our competition."

The old man in the wheelchair watched his screen intensely as two red dots moved through a complex grid. "They're heading west, back into town," he said into his ear piece, giving orders to Hans and Frederick to do the same.

"They got away?" Mr. Trick asked as he looked over toward the screen.

"Temporarily."

A grin came over Mr. Trick's face. "Give it up for

the slayers. They got character." Suddenly there was a loud, forceful knock at the door. "I'll take care of it," Mr. Trick told the old man.

When he opened the door, Mr. Trick came face-to-face with four uniformed officers from the Sunnydale Police Department. "Evening gentlemen. How may I help you?" he asked, ever the gracious host.

The police responded by grabbing him and dragging them to their squad car. "Excuse me," Mr. Trick demanded. "Anybody have a warrant here?"

It wasn't easy trekking down the highway at night in stiletto heels, but Buffy and Cordelia finally made their way back to Sunnydale High. As they walked down an empty hallway, Buffy made a mental list of just where each of their attackers were located at that moment. "Jungle Bob and Spikehead are down," she recalled. "We lost the Germans twice, but they seem to keep finding us. We take out them and the Gorches, we can still make it to homecoming."

Cordelia nodded in agreement. Amazingly enough, she didn't realize just how ludicrous that statement seemed. After all, she and Buffy weren't exactly stylin' anymore. Their dresses were shredded, their faces were filthy with dirt and soot, and their hairstyles were complete disasters. To top it all off, Cordelia was still clutching the spatula.

Still, their corsages seemed to be in good shape.

"Those animals," Cordelia said with indignation in her voice. "Hunting us down like poor defenseless . . . well, animals, I guess."

Buffy pushed open the door of the library. "Now we just need—"

Before the Slayer could finish her sentence, Candy Gorch kicked her hard in the stomach slamming her against a shelf of books. Buffy was caught completely off guard. The newlywed vamp got a few more good kicks and punches in before Buffy even knew what hit her.

But Cordelia was unharmed.

"Buffy!" Cordelia tossed her spatula in the Slayer's direction. Buffy grabbed held the spatula like a stake, and aimed it straight for Candy's heart. The tool met its mark, but not before the vamp was able to slam Buffy to the ground with an old coat rack.

"Candy!" Lyle Gorch watched in horror as his wife dissolved into dust. He bent down and picked up her pink barrette from the pile of powdery ash. The anger burned through his hideous face. "First ma brother Tector, now ma wife." He lunged toward Buffy, who now lay unconscious on the ground beside her Watcher. "I'll kill ya for this, Slayer!" Then he turned to Cordelia. "You too!" the vamp swore, as his face turned red with fury. "You're dead meat. Ya hear? I'm gonna . . ."

Cordelia looked from Buffy to Giles. They were both still unconscious. This was up to her. "I know, rip out my innards, play with my eyeballs, boil my brain and eat it for brunch," Cordy suggested in a voice that was decidedly unimpressed. She stared angrily at the vampire. "Now listen up, needle-brain. Buffy and I have taken out four of your cronies, not to mention your girlfriend—"

"Wife!" Lyle Gorch corrected her.

"Whatever. The point is, I haven't even worked up a sweat." Cordelia took a step closer, getting right into the vamp's ugly face. "See in the end, Buffy's good, but she's just the runner-up. I'm the queen. You get me mad, what do you think I'm gonna do?"

Something in Cordelia's eyes let Lyle know that he was completely out of his league. He looked from Cordy to Buffy to the pile of dust that used to be his Candy. "Later!" he exclaimed as he carefully backed out of the door.

Slowly Giles opened his eyes and struggled to his feet. From what he'd heard through his semi-conscious fog, this Homecoming Queen candidate had just put on an amazing performance.

Buffy wasn't quite sure how long she'd been unconscious. But when she came to, Giles made sure to tell her about Cordelia's courageous act. Despite the fact that they were competitors and that she currently was nursing one mother of a splitting headache, Buffy had to admit that Cordy had done a helluva job.

"Teach 'em to mistake you for a slayer," Buffy congratulated her.

Giles became slightly uncomfortable. "I feel somewhat to blame for that," he apologized to Buffy and Cordelia. "I did give your friends tacit approval to pull the switch in the limousine."

"Nah, that's okay," Buffy assured him. "Cor and I spent some quality death time."

"And we got these free corsages," Cordelia reminded her.

"Nice," Giles replied. "Although I don't recall them saying anything about corsages." Immediately he and Buffy both took a second look at the flowers the girls were wearing.

"Jungle Bob said the Germans were hooked into a computer system," Buffy mused out loud as she examined her corsage. She pulled back a petal. Funny, her bio teacher had never mentioned a computer chip when discussing the parts of a plant. "And they're hooked into us."

Suddenly the trio heard a door slam loudly in the outer hallway. Cordelia ripped off her corsage and tossed it at Buffy. "Oh, God! Get rid of these things," she exclaimed.

Buffy turned to Giles. "I'll need some wet toilet paper."

"Oh, yeah. That'll help," Cordelia said sarcastically, not knowing what Buffy was thinking.

As Buffy formulated her plan to set Frederick and Hans off the track, the old man in the mansion was documenting the girls' every move.

"I have them. Axis six degrees by forty-three," he transmitted to the German fighters as he watched the red dots move across his screen.

Quickly Hans rounded the corner, just as Buffy dashed across the hall to a nearby classroom. In the darkness, Hans did not see Buffy—or the wadded up ball of wet toilet paper she was holding, which was wrapped around the two corsages. Buffy reached back and then pitched the flowers like a baseball across the room. *Splat!* They hit their target, sticking squarely onto Hans's back. He didn't feel a thing.

"Transmitting coordinates now. They're fifty feet away," the old man reported into his headpiece, his voice becoming more excited as his prey seemed to be breathing their last. "Both targets axis six by forty-three." He stared at the screen as the two red dots appeared to merge into one. "I have them both in range together. Twenty feet and stationary. Locked into final position. Fire when ready!"

Hans turned slowly and readied his gun. Frederick, waiting in the next classroom, did the same. "Both targets seven degrees by thirty-five," the old man told them. "Adjust by ten degrees. FIRE!"

Frederick fired his gun. The bullet blasted straight through the classroom wall. Hans heard the gun go off and instinctively returned the fire. Suddenly there was a gun battle going on between the two classrooms. The wall between the brothers kept them from seeing that they were actually shooting at one another. And both thought they were killing the slayers.

In an instant it was all over. Hans and Frederick lay dead on the floor of their respective classrooms. The old man stared at his computer screen and watched as the red dots disappeared from view.

"I won!" he declared in disbelief.

Buffy and Cordelia were more concerned with who had won a different type of contest. Once they had defeated their enemies, the girls hurried to get to the Bronze, hoping to get there in time to see if they had defeated each other.

As they traveled across town, the girls had no idea that the mayor of Sunnydale was busy entertaining the vampire who was responsible for their current disheveled appearance.

"Hello. Nice to meet you," the Mayor said as two of his officers dragged Mr. Trick into his office.

"Yeah, pleasure," Mr. Trick snarled. "Where am I?"

The Mayor smiled. "In my office. I'm Richard Wilkins, mayor of Sunnydale. And you're Mr. Trick. Please sit down." The Mayor watched as Mr. Trick sat in a chair across the desk. "That's an exciting suit."

Mr. Trick opened his suit jacket to give the Mayor a better look. "Clothes make the man."

"As I understand it, you're not a man *exactly*," the Mayor remarked, never once ceasing his political smile. Mr. Trick nodded, but said nothing. "I've been mayor for sometime," the Mayor continued. "I like things to run smoothly. This is a very important year for me."

"An election year," Mr. Trick guessed.

"Something like that," the Mayor agreed.

"This is the part where you say that I don't fit in in your quiet little neighborhood?" Mr. Trick asked accusingly. "You can skip it. That all got old long before I became a vampire. Do you know what I'm saying?"

The Mayor shook his head. "The children are the heart of a community. They need to be looked after, controlled," the Mayor explained. "The more rebellious elements need to be dealt with. The children are our future. We need them. *I* need them."

Mr. Trick smiled. "If this 'rebellious element' means what I think it does, then this problem may be taken care of this very night."

Now Mayor Wilkins's smile seemed almost genuine. "So I've heard. That's a very enterprising idea you've had. Slayerfest. I love that name, by the way." He laughed. "You see, that's the kind of initiative I see on my team."

Mr. Trick did not return the Mayor's smile. "What if I don't want to be a part of the team?"

Mayor Wilkins shook his head. "Oh, no, that won't be an issue," he assured Mr. Trick.

The Bronze looked almost magical to Buffy, with silver streamers and huge, brightly colored banners covering the walls. Buffy grinned. It was nice to be at a dance again—even if she was sort of disheveled. *Make that a total mess.*

As Devon, a hot-looking senior, took the stage with envelope in hand, Willow began to get nervous. "They're gonna announce the queen. Where are they? What's keeping them?"

Xander turned just in time to see the candidates in question walk into the room. One look at their filthy faces, and all he could say was, "I'm gonna go with mud wrestling. My God, what did you two do to each other?" he added as the two girls made their way over to where he, Willow, Oz, Faith, and Giles were standing.

"Long story," Buffy replied.

"Got hunted," Cordelia explained.

"Apparently not that long," Buffy corrected herself.

Then she smiled slightly. "I'll tell you, though. You don't ever want to mess with Cordelia."

That was a lesson Xander had already learned. "No," he agreed.

Devon took his place by the microphone and held up the small white envelope. "In this envelope I hold the name of this year's Homecoming Queen."

Cordelia looked over at Buffy. "You know, after all we've been through tonight, this whole who-gets-to-be-queen-capade seems pretty—"

"Damn important," Buffy finished her sentence.

"Oh, yeah!" Cordelia agreed, as she focused her attention back at the stage.

"And the winner is . . ." Devon tore the envelope open in one quick step. He looked surprised. "Hey! I believe this is a first for Sunnydale High. We have a tie."

Buffy and Cordelia stood side-by-side. Their hearts were beating so quickly that each was sure the other could hear hers.

"Holly Charleston and Michelle Blake!" Devon shouted out.

At first, Cordy wasn't sure she'd heard correctly. But as Holly and Michelle tearfully made their way to the stage, there was no denying what had just happened.

Buffy and Cordy turned in unison and headed for the door. There was no point in sticking around.

Epilogue

Cordelia spotted the sign the second she walked in the front door of the Bronze. The huge banner was still on the stage, hanging right behind the house band.

The homecoming party—or as Cordelia liked to call it, The Homecoming from Hell—had been over for a week. For the most part, the Bronze was back to its normal state—dismal lighting, sticky floors, and poor service. In fact the only sign that homecoming had been held there was that hideous banner hanging behind the stage. Some moron had obviously forgotten to take it down.

Actually, much to her surprise, the lack of a tiara on her head hadn't really affected Cordelia's life at all. Rhinestone-covered aluminum crowns don't come in all that handy when you're slaying vamps or kicking monster butt.

A spatula's much better for that. Cordelia grinned, remembering. She glanced over at Buffy, with whom she'd spent the entire homecoming evening slaying vampires and monsters—and enjoying it, in an empowerment kind of way.

Cordelia Chase hanging out with a freakazoid like Buffy Summers . . . and liking it? Okay, *that* was plenty weird. But stranger still was the idea that the Slayerfest had forced Cordy to miss her date with the man of her dreams: *Xander Harris*.

One thing was for sure, senior year wasn't turning out the way Cordelia would have predicted. But as Xander came up and pecked her on the cheek, Cordy smiled contentedly. *Unpredictablity is what makes it all so exciting.*